To Sarah
Great

HORSE CRAZY!

The Complete Adventures of BONNIE and SAM

Alison Lester
pictures by Roland Harvey

ALLEN&UNWIN

Sophie J

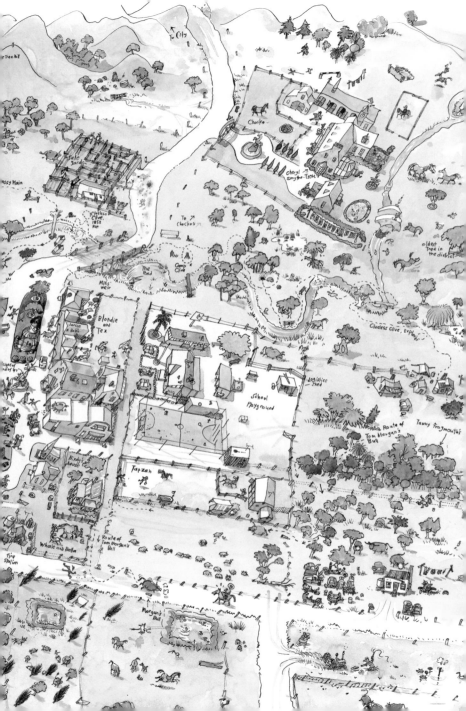

Alison Lester would like to thank Charlie, Joan and Rob
for information about sheep and abalone for *Racing the Tide*,
and Kath Burton, Kerry Delaney and Sandy Anderson
for stories about the show for *Saving Mr Pinto*.

First published in 2009

Allen & Unwin
83 Alexander St
Crows Nest NSW 2065
Australia
Phone: (61 2) 8425 0100
Fax: (61 2) 9906 2218
Email: info@allenandunwin.com
Web: www.allenandunwin.com

National Library of Australia
Cataloguing-in-Publication entry:
  Lester, Alison
  Bonnie & Sam horse-crazy! Alison Lester;
  illustrator, Roland Harvey
  ISBN 978 1 74175 830 6
  For primary school age
  Horses – Juvenile fiction
A823.3

Cover and text design by Sandra Nobes
Set in 14 pt Berkeley Oldstyle by Tou-Can Design
Printed in China through Colorcraft Ltd, Hong Kong

10 9 8 7 6 5 4 3 2 1

www.bonnieandsam.com.au

Contents

BONNIE and SAM
The Shadow Brumby

For my horsey friend Evie A.L.
For Annabel, for the horse poses R.H.

Bonnie and Sam

Bonnie and Sam knew all the horses and ponies in Currawong Creek. They were **horse-crazy!**

Sam's real name was Samantha. She lived with her dad, Bill, in an old house that overlooked the creek. Bill Cooper was the local policeman.

Sam

Bonnie

Pants

Bonnie – Bon for short – lived just outside town on a huge farm called Peppermint Plain. Bon's parents weren't interested in horses, even though Peppermint Plain was the perfect place for riding. Her mum, Woo, was a painter, always busy in her studio. Her dad, Chester, loved riding around the farm on his motorbike.

But Bonnie and Sam lived for horses.

Bonnie could talk a special horse language that she was sure they understood.

Sam was strong and horsey. She could tell, just by looking at a horse, if it had a stone in its hoof or needed a drink.

Sam's dog, Pants, followed her everywhere. Pants was short for Smartie Pants, because she thought she knew everything.

The Horses and Ponies of Currawong Creek

Bonnie and Sam didn't have a horse of their own, but they managed to ride nearly every day.

Their favourite horse was Whale, who belonged to Bon's Aunty Birdy. Whale was huge. He was long and wide and tall. He was so broad that Bonnie and Sam could sit face-to-face and play poker on his back.

Whale shared his paddock with Bella, a tiny skewbald pony whose mane came down to her knees. When Sam sat on Bella, she could reach the ground with both big toes. Bella had been Bonnie's first pony, but the girls were far too big to ride her now. Instead, they spent hours grooming her and plaiting her mane.

Whale

Bella

Then there was Biscuit, the most
neglected horse in Currawong Creek.
Wally Webster, the stock agent, hated horses
but he needed poor Biscuit for his stock work.
If Bonnie and Sam hadn't checked her feed and
water every day, she would have died long ago.
Biscuit was frightened of Wally's rough ways and
bellowing voice, so Wally depended on the girls
to catch her for him. In return, they could ride
her whenever they wanted.

Biscuit

Chocolate Charme was another favourite.
Her owner, Cheryl Smythe-Tyght, lived near
the saleyards on a property that looked like a
toy farm. It had perfect white fences, red sheds,
and neat rows of trees with every leaf in place.
Chocko was a dressage horse: beautiful, well-
educated and obedient. Sometimes Sam and
Bonnie picked up horse poo in Cheryl's paddocks
in exchange for riding lessons. Trotting around
Cheryl's ménage on the fabulous Chocko was the
closest thing to heaven the girls had ever known.

Then there were Blondie and Tex, who came to Currawong Creek when their owners, Janice and Bob, took over the newsagency.

Blondie was an elderly quarter horse with a butterscotch coat and a sparkling white mane and tail. Every now and then something would remind her of her sad past, and she'd go all nervous and spooky. Bon could whisper to Blondie in secret horse language and calm her down.

Tex was an ugly Appaloosa with a very sweet nature. He adored Blondie. Nothing bothered Tex, not even when Bob dressed him up as a reindeer last Christmas and threw presents to the little kids waiting outside the newsagency.

Blondie

Tex

Horrie

Prince Regent, known as Horrie, was
Currawong Creek's one and only racehorse.
He hadn't won a race for years, but his owner,
Bugsy Brady, believed he still had it in him.
Horrie was as scatty as a cat and saw spooks in
every shadow. Sometimes, Bon and Sam gave
him a neck massage on their way home from
school. It always put him to sleep.

Tricky was a piebald pony, with a black-and-white personality to match his colouring. He was either very, very good or very, very bad. At pony club, he often played tricks on Michael, his owner. Tricky was the best games pony around, as nimble as a monkey, but if he felt like playing up he was a disaster.

Tricky was devoted to Sam, who never walked past his paddock without stopping to adjust his fly veil or share her apple.

Tricky

The grumpiest pony in Currawong Creek was Tarzan. He was a shaggy buckskin who lived in the paddock next to the primary school. Children had teased him for so long that he chased anyone who came near. Only Sam was brave enough to stand her ground, with Bonnie hiding behind her. Tarzan knew that the girls always brought a treat to make him happy.

Bonnie and Sam could ride all the horses, often bareback and double-dinking. Whenever there was time, the girls borrowed a horse and went riding.

Sometimes in the mountains they caught a glimpse of the wild bush horses – the brumbies. They looked so wild and free, yet Sam and Bonnie couldn't help dreaming about catching a yearling and taming it.

What they didn't know was that one night, while they were still dreaming, a brumby would come to them ...

Tarzan

11

Drover

Sam sat on the back porch and watched her dad's new horse, Drover, pacing up and down the fence.

'Why's she so unhappy, Pants?'

The little dog whined softly, as if to say, *She's unhappy because she hates being locked up.*

Drover's head was turned towards the hills. You could tell she wanted to be there.

Sam called out, 'Drover! Dro-ver!' but the silver-grey mare didn't even look her way.

Pants rubbed against Sam's leg and made her special snuffly noises that meant, *Look at me! I want to be here.*

Sam scratched her wiry coat. 'I know you're happy. But Drover just wants to run away.'

The reason Drover hated being locked in a small paddock was that she had spent all her life on the open road. She was a drover's horse. Sam's dad had a mate called Smithy who caught Drover as a two-year-old brumby and broke her in. She grew up to be quick, clever and calm. Smithy loved her. But one night he camped near a railway line and Drover was nearly hit by a train. She wasn't hurt, but, after that night, every time she heard or saw a train, she bolted.

'She runs like the devil's after her,' Smithy explained when he brought Drover to Currawong Creek. 'I can't use her any more because I often work near a train line.'

Sam's heart did a little somersault. Maybe he was going to give the horse to her!

'But you could use her, Bill. There's no train line here. She'd be perfect for your police work. And her hard little hooves never need shoes.'

Sam's face dropped and Smithy guessed what she had been hoping.

'I'm sorry, Sam. I know you'd love your own horse, but this one's not for you. She's definitely not a kid's horse.'

Drover turned out to be an excellent police horse. Bill could catch her any time, day or night, and she'd do whatever he asked.

It didn't bother Bill that she was unfriendly and restless in her paddock. He just wanted a horse that did the job, and Drover did.

Together, Bill and Drover herded Wally Webster's sheep back into their paddock when they wandered through the town in the middle of the night. They did it so quietly that Mrs Green never knew what had eaten her roses and gladioli.

When Tom Morgan's bad-tempered bull went rampaging through town, Bill and Drover stopped him. Bill cracked his whip and Drover ducked away from the bull's fearsome horns. Together they forced the brute back to his yard.

And when Mrs Kowalski's kitten got stuck up a tree, Drover stood steady while Bill fetched her down.

'She's the best horse I've ever owned,' Bill said to Sam. 'I've had her for three weeks now and she hasn't put a foot wrong.'

But Drover wasn't a great horse for Bonnie and Sam.

One Saturday afternoon when Bill was away, they decided to ride her. The girls were used to all the Currawong Creek horses liking them. Not Drover. When she bucked Sam off, they thought Sam's jump-up had frightened her. But when Bonnie slid gently on from a stump, the same thing happened. A swish of mane, a stamp of hooves, and Bonnie was on the ground. The girls both tried until they were sore and sick of it.

'And look.' Bonnie went to hug Drover, but the mare pulled away. 'She doesn't even like us touching her.'

Sam pulled off her helmet and rubbed a grass stain on it. 'Smithy said she wasn't a kid's horse. Maybe she's only been ridden by a grown-up, and we seem a bit weird.'

'Maybe a kid did something mean and gave her that moon-shaped scar under her mane.'

Bonnie rolled up her trouser leg to inspect her own scar. 'Oh well, I guess it's like people. Not everyone wants to be your friend.'

Shadow

Late one night, Shadow the silver brumby slipped through the gum trees, racing to catch up with the mob.

She hated being last. Everywhere Shadow looked, she saw danger. The other wild horses trotted happily through the moonlit bush, but Shadow was afraid.

Shadow had been born on a farm where she felt safe and secure. Then one day her mother

pushed open a broken gate and took Shadow into the mountains, following the call of the brumbies. From then on, Shadow was always tense and worried.

Storms were Shadow's greatest fear. She hated the terrifying crash of thunder, and the lightning that tore through Wild Dog Range. Most of all, she hated being afraid.

Now the stallion who led the brumbies plunged down the mountain, scattering rocks, with the mob close behind. The smell of smoke and humans drifted through the trees. He was leading them to the town!

The brumbies trotted silently across the river flats. Lights glowed yellow through the mist and a dog barked, *Arf, arf, arf.* They slowed to a walk, reaching down to snatch bites of sweet green grass.

The stallion stopped still, quivering, ears forward. Then he pranced up to a fence and Shadow saw what had lured him from the mountains. A beautiful silver-grey mare stood neck-to-neck with the brumby stallion, breathing his scent.

That mare was Drover.

Suddenly the mare squealed and spun around, kicking. The stallion backed away and led his mob further along the creek. But Shadow stopped to stare at Drover. It was as though she were seeing her own reflection. They were identical.

The two silver-grey
mares moved to the fence,
like dancers coming together.
Shadow gazed into the paddock
with its shade trees, water trough
and stable, so comfortable and safe.
Drover looked past Shadow at the
brumbies grazing by the river, free
to race back to their wild mountain home.
Both horses saw the life they wanted, with
only the fence in their way.

The stallion trotted back from the creek, snorting and driving Shadow away. With a fierce cry he led the mob back into the hills, leaving Drover alone in her paddock.

The sound of the wild horses disappearing into the bush made Drover feel as if she were in jail. Her hooves kicked up tiny puffs of dust as she paced along the fence. Her ears strained to hear the brumbies. One set of hoof beats sounded strangely close... closer... Then, like a ghost appearing from darkness, Shadow burst out of the night and trotted up to Drover.

Neck-to-neck they stood, nuzzling each other's withers. Then Shadow wheeled away, cantered back and flew over the fence like a bird.

Drover's heart lifted as the brumby jumped into her paddock. It looked so easy, so effortless. She knew she could do it too.

Shadow and Drover danced together, twisting and spinning in the moonlight. If Sam had looked out of her bedroom window just then, she would have thought she was dreaming.

The horses cantered in a circle, side-by-side. Then Shadow peeled away while Drover raced straight for the fence, soared over with room to spare, whinnied, and galloped away into the night.

Shadow turned and looked around her new paddock. She gave a sigh and felt a delicious peace come over her. She was home.

New Drover

Bill Cooper finished his cup of tea and glanced down the paddock. 'Look, Drover's finally stopped pacing up and down! I don't believe it. She's snoozing by the shed.'

Sam and Bonnie went to see if Drover really had calmed down. They walked slowly, calling her name and softly holding out an apple as a peace offering. The horse stared at them, head up, snorting, eyes nearly popping out of her head.

'What's happened to her?' Bon was puzzled. 'She normally just ignores us, but she's acting as if we're Martians. Look, she's trembling like a leaf.'

The mare didn't turn her rump to them in her usual unfriendly way. Instead, she moved forwards slowly. Then, very cautiously, she nuzzled Bon's neck.

Bon giggled and put her arms around the mare's neck. Drover leant into her as though she loved it.

'This is very weird,' said Sam, rubbing the horse's ears. 'She looks the same, but she's behaving so different.'

Bon put her nose right on Drover's grey coat and sniffed. 'She even smells different. She smells of the bush.'

The two girls went over the horse like detectives, looking for clues. They found that, overnight, Bill's horse had developed a matted mane and tail, cracked hooves and a couple of new scars on her legs. The crescent-shaped scar under her mane had disappeared.

'You're not Drover,' said Bon, shaking her head. 'You're somebody else!'

'I'd better tell Dad.'

'Hang on, Sammy.' Bon was untangling the mare's mane. 'She loves us. Maybe we shouldn't tell him. Drover was never this friendly.'

'She is nice,' Sam agreed, 'but Dad's bound to find out anyway. Look at her hooves.'

'We could trim them, and comb the knots out of her mane. He'll never notice.'

'But who swapped her? It's not fair on Dad. They must think he's too stupid to know his own horse.'

'Mmmnn, that's something to think about.'
Bon crinkled up her eyes the way she always did
when she had a problem. 'Let's check the bottom
fence.'

The mare followed, nudging them gently with
her nose. They expected to find the fence cut,
but it looked the same as ever.

Sam wriggled carefully through the barbed
wire and bent down, studying the ground. 'A
lot of horses have been here, and none of them
were wearing shoes.' She looked at Bon proudly.
'You know what that means?'

'Brumbies! Maybe Drover has gone off with
the brumbies. And maybe this horse is a
brumby who decided to stay. Oh, please don't
tell your dad, Sam, not right away anyhow.
Let's just see how she turns out.'

The Makeover

The new Drover was a quick learner. She stood as still as stone while Bonnie and Sam took turns with the big hoof rasp. They filed off the broken bits until the new mare's hooves were as smooth and round as the old Drover's.

Everything was new to her. As the day went by, the girls became more and more convinced that their 'brumby swap' theory was right.

When they put a headstall on her, she snorted and looked surprised, but didn't back away. Whenever she seemed afraid, Bonnie soothed her with secret horse talk and massaged the tension out of her neck. They combed all the knots out of her mane and tail, then trimmed the bottom of her tail square, like they'd done with old Drover. Then they washed her and brushed her as she dried in the sunshine.

'I don't think your dad will be able to tell the difference.' Bon stared at their handiwork from the shade of the old gum tree. 'She looks just the same.'

'Yep.' Sam fondled Pants's ears. 'She *looks* the same. But when he rides her, he'll notice.'

Bonnie and Sam decided they needed help. An unbroken brumby would be hard to train, no matter how friendly she was. They called on someone they could trust – Birdy Davidson. Aunty Birdy never treated them like little kids, and she knew everything there was to know about horses.

When the girls told her about Drover and the brumby, she nodded. 'It sounds as though you're right about the swap. Horses have a mind of their own, you know.'

The three of them sat on the bench on the verandah and watched Birdy's horse Whale grazing in the paddock behind the house.

'Can you tell us how to train her?' Bon asked. 'She won't know anything about being ridden.'

Sam squirmed in her chair. She still didn't feel good about tricking her father.

'We've only got five days. Dad always rides through the town on Thursdays. And it takes ages to break in a horse, doesn't it?'

'Well, it depends on the horse,' answered
Birdy. 'Look at Whale. He's such a sweet-natured
horse that he almost trained himself. Your
brumby sounds the same. Let's go and have a
look at her.'

Over the next five days, whenever Bill Cooper was away from home, Birdy and the girls worked on the new Drover.

On the first day they taught her to lead. Sam walked beside the mare, gently encouraging her forwards. When Sam stopped, Drover stopped. When Sam walked, she walked too. Then Sam ran slowly and the brumby trotted beside her.

Birdy smiled. She liked the look of this horse and her gentle eye. 'Now make her go backwards,' she said to Sam. 'It's important she knows to yield to you.'

Sam held the rope close to the headstall and pushed steadily away. Drover stepped carefully back. 'Good girl,' soothed Sam. 'Good horse.'

On the second day they taught her to tie up and accept the saddle. Sam put the saddle blanket on Drover's back, then carefully placed Bill's heavy stock saddle on top. Drover jumped slightly and then looked embarrassed. Her reactions were the same with every step: at first she was frightened, but she quickly took to things.

On the third day they put her bridle on. She mouthed the bit at first as though she'd tasted something really bad, but soon started chewing on it. 'That's good,' said Birdy. 'That means she's accepted it.'

On the fourth day they drove her in long reins, making sure she knew which way to go and when to stop.

On the fifth day it was time to get on. When Sam swung up into the saddle, new Drover turned her head and stared in amazement. Bon patted her neck and soothed her, then Sam squeezed her legs and the horse stepped forwards. Birdy and Bon watched them go around the paddock, walking, circling left, circling right, sideways, backwards.

Finally Sam pushed Drover into a canter. They turned and trotted back up to where Birdy and Bon were sitting. Sam swung out of the saddle. She was beaming.

'She's beautiful, isn't she? Have a ride, Bon, you'll love her. I think she's going to be okay.'

Test Drive

The next day, Bill got ready for his weekly tour of the town.

'Please don't do anything stupid,' Sam whispered into new Drover's ear.

Drover gave a little snort of surprise as Bill swung into the saddle and his full weight settled on her back.

Bill turned to ride out the gate and Drover didn't respond. Old Drover would have felt the shift of his body and moved off, but new Drover just stood still. Bill had to squeeze with his legs to make her go. Sam quickly went to her head and led her through the gate.

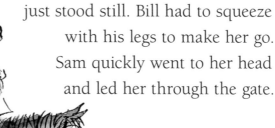

'What's gotten into her?' said Bill. 'She's acting like a drongo.' He turned the mare towards the town and kicked her forwards. Sam crossed her fingers.

'Have a lovely ride, Dad. Don't fall off.' Sam bit her lip. 'He thinks I'm joking,' she said to Pants.

Sergeant Bill Cooper loved riding through town. It was a good way to keep in touch with people. He saw all sorts of things from the back of his horse that he'd never see from his car. He always took the same route, so nobody thought he was sneaking around. But today, his horse's mind was not on the job. She wobbled and weaved as though she had no idea where she was going, and stared at everything. Bill had to ride her like a green horse that knew nothing.

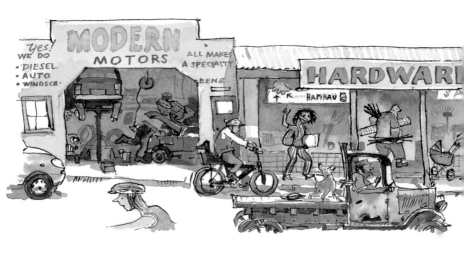

'Hey, Bill!' Mick Daly, the baker, called from over the street. 'I want to ask you something.'

Bill steered Drover across, expecting her to stop just in front of Mick. But Drover walked right up close until Mick's face was pressed against her mane.

'Whoa there, horse,' said Mick, stepping back. 'Hasn't she heard about personal space?'

'I don't know what the story is, mate. She's acting very strangely.'

The two men chatted for a while, but, when
Mick walked back inside his bakery, Drover
followed him right into the shop. Bill had to
duck quickly to fit under the doorway. Drover
stopped at the counter and Bill looked down at
Mrs Bowman, who was putting a poppy-seed
loaf into her shopping trolley.

'I don't think the health inspector would
approve of a horse in a food store,' Mrs Bowman
sniffed. 'Even a police horse.' She minced out of
the shop with her trolley, and Mick burst out
laughing.

'It's pretty funny, Bill, but you'd better get her
out of here. I could be fined.'

'I might not be able to keep her after all, Sam,' said Bill, watching the mare roll in the paddock after the ride. 'She's been such a good horse until now, but today she was a real dodo.'

Sam wanted to tell her dad the truth right then, but it was such a big thing to confess. When he told her all the odd things Drover had done, her heart sank.

'Did you laugh when she ate the flowers on Mrs Milson's hat?' she asked, hanging up the bridle.

'I wanted to. But I had to be serious. I'm the policeman. And I've got a horse that's breaking the law.' He picked up Pants and scratched her back. 'The trouble is, I don't know if I can trust her. Next weekend I have to take her to the Baxter Show. They want a mounted officer there, and Charlie Craig's horse is lame.'

He put Pants down, stretched and yawned.

'I wish she hadn't started acting so strangely, just when I have to put her to the test. The train line goes through Baxter, right near the showgrounds. What if she freaks out at the 2.30 train?'

Sam patted her dad on the back. 'She'll be fine, Dad. I bet you anything she won't worry about the train.'

She hurried inside to ring Bonnie. This new Drover might do some weird things, but she had no reason to be scared of trains.

The Baxter Show

Bonnie and Sam led Drover past the ferris wheel and the dodgem cars. Bonnie talked to her all the time in her secret horse language. The mare was calm, although she looked wide-eyed at all the action going on around her. People kept stopping to admire her beautiful silver-grey coat.

'We're taking her to meet my dad at the cattle sheds,' Sam explained for the eighth time.

Drover took a bite from a little boy's fairy floss and Sam and Bonnie quickly led her on.

'I hope she'll be okay, Bon,' said Sam. 'It would be terrible if something went wrong because of what we've done.'

'She'll be fine. Now she knows your dad, she'll be much better. Look! There he is!'

Bonnie and Sam sat on the arena fence, watching the dressage horses go round and round. Chocolate Charme was in the final for Champion Hack of the Show. She moved through her work-out like a well-oiled Rolls Royce, her brown coat shining in the sun, saddlery gleaming. The girls clapped and cheered when the red, white and blue champion sash was put around Chocko's neck.

They were heading for the arena exit when a siren suddenly howled over the loudspeaker.

'Sergeant Bill Cooper! Calling Sergeant Bill Cooper! We have an emergency! Come straight to the tent in the main arena.'

Sam watched her father gallop across the ground. 'She's going good for him, Bonnie.'

It was true, the mare did seem calm and confident.

'You have to help us!' A desperate woman rushed towards Bill. Her eyes were red from crying. 'Our little girl has disappeared. She was right beside me, on her trike, and then all of a sudden she was gone!'

Bill quickly took down the details and organised a message over the loudspeaker.

'We have a missing child at the Baxter Showgrounds. Kimberley Mills is two years old and was riding her red plastic tricycle near the ferris wheel when she disappeared. She has blonde curly hair and is wearing purple overalls

and a white tee shirt. I repeat, we have a missing child…'

Bill raced away to search for the little girl. Suddenly there was a scream from behind the showground toilets.

Bill galloped Drover around the tumbledown building and there was Kimberley's mother, pointing into the distance. 'There she is!'

Behind a hedge of blackberries was a laneway, and right at the end of the lane was a small purple figure.

'Can you see? That's her! I know it's her!'

'You'd better be quick,' said an elderly man. 'The railway line's at the end of that lane.'

Bill felt suddenly afraid. 'Railway line? Oh, no.' He looked at his watch. 'There's a train coming in five minutes!'

Bill rode Drover up to the blackberry hedge. He had no choice but to jump it. Nobody on foot could reach the little girl in time. He didn't think Drover had ever jumped anything as big and rough as this hedge. He cantered back a short way, turned, and set the mare at the tangled barrier.

Bonnie and Sam had raced to the toilets when they heard the scream. A crowd followed behind them. They came around the corner just as Bill and Drover galloped at the hedge.

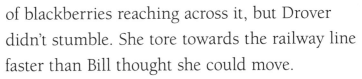

'Go, Dad!' Sam yelled, as Drover flew over the blackberries.

The mare raced down the laneway. The ground was rough and rutted, with snarls of blackberries reaching across it, but Drover didn't stumble. She tore towards the railway line faster than Bill thought she could move.

From close by came the *whooo hooo!* of the train.

'Come on, girl,' Bill said to Drover. 'Don't freak out at the train. I need you to be brave.'

It seemed to take for ever to reach the railway line. Each time the train whistled, Bill felt a cold hand clasp his heart. Suddenly Drover turned so fast that Bill had to hang on with everything he had.

He could see Kimberley ahead of him! She had pushed her trike onto the train tracks and was kicking it along with her chubby little legs.

Whooo hooo!

Bill glanced over his shoulder as Drover leapt up onto the tracks. The train was coming, closer and closer. Surely the driver could see him.

'Kimberley!' he shouted. 'Get off the track!'

The toddler turned at the sound of her name and Bill shuddered to see how helpless she was. He urged Drover forwards. Behind him, he could hear the squeal of the train's brakes.

The little girl looked up in terror as the horse galloped towards her.

Drover didn't shy away. It was as though she knew exactly what Bill needed to do. Bill leant out of the saddle, way out and down. As Drover galloped past, he grabbed Kimberley by the back of her purple corduroy overalls and lifted her to safety.

Drover veered off the train tracks, scrambling down the bank like a cat, and slowed to a canter, then a stop, as the train roared safely past.

The train driver was leaning out his window, looking back. Bill gave him a wave to let him know everything was all right.

The little girl hadn't uttered a sound, but now she said, 'Horsey.'

'That's right,' said Bill, settling her on the pommel of his saddle. 'She's a wonderful horsey.'

He could hear the cheer from the crowd at the showgrounds as soon as they turned down the lane. Drover walked quietly, sides heaving after the gallop. Kimberley babbled and laughed. Her parents raced towards them and Bill passed the little girl down. It was only then that he realised she was still sitting on her trike. When he'd scooped her up, she had held on to the plastic handlebars, and the trike had come with her.

Kimberley's parents kissed her and cuddled her, inspected her for cuts and scratches, and thanked Bill over and over. They walked back along the laneway to the showgrounds, with Bill following on Drover. Kimberley kept turning in her father's arms, calling, 'Horsey, horsey,' until finally they passed her up to Bill and she rode into the cheering crowd like a little princess.

A voice yelled out, 'Three cheers for Bill Cooper!' and everybody cheered him. Then someone else yelled, 'And three cheers for the horse!' and they cheered Drover, too.

The Truth

Sam tried to tell her father the truth about Drover that night. She lay on their saggy couch with Pants on her lap and listened as Bill told Smithy how brave his horse had been.

'She's been acting weird this week,' he said into the phone. 'It was like she'd forgotten everything she'd ever learnt. I thought I might have to get rid of her, but, mate, you should have seen her today. What a star. She galloped in front of that train as cool as a cucumber.'

He held the phone away from his ear and grinned at Sam as Smithy's squawks of disbelief echoed down the line.

'I don't know what's changed her, but thank you. Thank you for a fantastic horse.' Bill leant back and stretched. 'Yeah, you take care out on the road. We'll see you in the spring. Bye, mate.'

'It's a different horse, Dad.' The words were
out of Sam's mouth before she'd even decided to
say them. 'This Drover is a brumby.'

Bill looked down at his socks for a moment
and then he roared with laughter. 'Ha, ha, Sam.
Very funny. My word, you're a tricker. You had
me thinking there for a minute. Come on, let's
get you into bed. It's been a huge day.'

One Year Later...

It was the first day of the summer holidays and it had rained for hours. Sam and Bonnie spent the whole afternoon inside, working on their horse scrapbooks. Bonnie drew a beautiful picture of the two of them double-dinking on Drover, and Sam wrote their names underneath. They rode the mare together all the time now, when Bill wasn't using her.

'I'm sick of being inside, Sam.' Bonnie walked across to the window. 'And look. It's stopped raining. Let's go for a ride.'

The sun was just starting to set and the evening light made everything glow. Drover trotted up to meet them and Sam slipped the bridle over her ears.

'Remember how snooty the old Drover was?' Bonnie said as she rubbed the mare's ears. 'Not like you, Miss Beautiful.'

Drover seemed to smile, as though she understood. Maybe Bonnie really could talk Horse.

Sam swung up onto Drover's back, then held her foot out rigid so Bon could use it as a step. Drover's coat was still damp after the rain, and the girls felt as though they were glued to her. They rode down to the creek, with Pants scouting ahead. Then they broke into an easy canter and loped out of town, leaving the little brown-and-white dog behind.

Drover's canter was smooth and unhurried, and they let her choose her own way. She turned up a bush track that wound into the foothills of Wild Dog Range. Her stride quickened.

'We'd better not go too far,' said Sam. 'Dad will go nuts if we're not home by dark.'

Suddenly the track opened into a small grassed valley surrounded by towering mountain ash trees, their pale trunks ragged with bark. Drover stopped still, listening, then whinnied. Her neigh rang around the clearing like a siren.

'She's calling the brumbies,' Bonnie whispered into Sam's ear. 'Maybe she wants to go back to them.'

Drover's ears were pricked, quivering. From high above came the noise of creatures moving fast through the bush. A whinny floated down. They could hear the horses getting closer. Then, there they were, on the far side of the valley,

twelve brumbies standing nervously together in
the evening gloom.

Drover felt liked a coiled spring under the
girls, as though she might explode in an instant.

'I'm scared, Sam,' Bonnie whispered. 'Do you
think we should get off?'

'No, we'll be okay. Relax. Trust her. Remember,
she chose to live with us. I don't think she wants
to go back to the mountains.'

A silver-grey horse stepped away from the mob and moved towards them.

'I bet that's old Drover,' Sam whispered so quietly that Bon only just caught her words. 'It's gotta be, don't you think?'

Bon squeezed Sam's waist. 'Look! She's got a foal.'

The mare came right up to them, nickering softly. The two silvery horses stood shoulder to shoulder, sniffing each other. Sam leant slowly across and lifted the brumby's mane. It was tangled, now, after a year in the bush. The moon-shaped scar showed dark against the silver coat.

'It is her! It's Dad's old Drover.'

Bonnie squeezed Sam so hard she couldn't breathe. 'Now we know for sure. Our horse detective theory is right!'

The brumbies suddenly turned back into the bush and old Drover wheeled to chase them. Her dark foal followed at her side.

Bonnie and Sam sat on their Drover, the horse that had chosen not to be a brumby, and listened to the wild horses moving off through the bush.

'We'd better go,' Bonnie said in a tiny voice. But before Sam even gathered the reins, Drover turned away from her old life and headed back along the track towards home.

All the house lights were on as they cantered through Currawong Creek. Anyone looking out would have seen only blackness, but Bonnie's and Sam's eyes were used to the dark. They raced up the track to Sam's house, night riders with a secret.

BONNIE and SAM
the Circus Pony

For Jenny A.L.
For Coco: hope your saddle is comfy R.H.

One Hot Afternoon

Bonnie and Sam knew all the horses and ponies in Currawong Creek. They were **horse-crazy!**

In summer, the friends always ended the school week with an icy pole at the milk bar.

They loved reading the posters in the window. It was the town noticeboard. If you had guinea pigs to spare or a computer to sell, that's where you'd advertise.

This Friday, the window was full.

'What if we found a *Free to a good home* ad for a beautiful horse?' said Sam. 'Wouldn't that be – '

'Look!' Bonnie cut in. 'There's a circus coming here in two weeks. Circo's Circus.'

'Hey, even better,' said Sam, 'the fire brigade's running a Talent Night again. Remember when Wally Webster's performing sheep pooed all over the stage?'

'What's the prize?' Bonnie read down the poster. 'A video camera for first and a digital camera for second! Third is two hundred photos printed free.'

'Wouldn't you love a video, Bon?' said Sam. 'We could take it with us when we ride up into the mountains. We could film the brumbies. Let's think of something fantastic to do.'

'Okay. We've got one week to find out what we're good at.'

Horses of
Currawong Creek

Most of the horses in Currawong Creek were looked after by their owners, some better than others. Sam made a point of checking them every day on her way to and from school. Bon often helped her instead of going home to Peppermint Plain on the school bus.

Tricky belonged to Michael Milton, the bossiest boy in the school. Tricky and Michael were the best combination in the pony club games team. They whizzed around barrels and poles so fast that Tricky's black-and-white patches blurred together. But apart from games, Michael ignored Tricky completely. His mother was so sick of nagging him to care for his horse that when Bonnie and Sam offered to do it she quickly said yes.

'Michael doesn't even like you,' Bonnie
whispered as Tricky rubbed his head against her
back. 'He just uses you like a motorbike.'

Sam turned on the tap to fill the water trough.
'Well, Tricky doesn't like him, either. He loves
us best, don't you, boy?'

Another horse they checked every day was Biscuit, a nervous chestnut mare who belonged to Wally Webster, the local stock agent. They gave her a quick rub and adjusted her fly veil, then headed for Sam's house. It was too hot to stay outside.

Sam's little dog Pants came to meet them, bouncing up and down on all four paws to make them laugh.

Bon loved coming home to Sam's empty house. Sam's dad, Bill, was the local policeman, so he was never around in the afternoon. The girls sat on the shady back verandah, drinking cold cordial from the fridge and eating chocolate teddy-bear biscuits.

'Hey, Drover!' Sam called to her father's grey mare who was dozing in the shade of the big gum tree. Drover pricked one ear, but she was too lazy to move.

Bonnie and Sam knew a secret that only one other person, Bonnie's Aunty Birdy, knew. Drover was once a brumby, a wild horse, living in the mountains. When she swapped places with Bill's old horse, Birdy had helped the girls teach her to be a policeman's horse. Drover loved the girls, and they rode her nearly every day.

When Bill came home, he reminded Sam that she was going to visit her cousins in the city. 'I'll run you back to Peppermint Plain, Bon, while Sam gets her things together. You can catch up with each other on Sunday.'

Bored

On Saturday morning, Bonnie tried to think up
an act for the Talent Night while she waited for
her mum. They were supposed to be going fishing
for yabbies in the big dam. But Woo was a painter,
and once she started on a new picture there was
no stopping her, no matter what she'd promised.

By late afternoon the painting was far from
finished. Bonnie tried everything – begging,
pleading, sooking, even a mini tantrum – but she
might as well have been performing to a fridge.

Finally Bonnie gave up and started flipping through art books. The afternoon sun and her mum's painting noises, mixed with music from the radio, made her sleepy.

Suddenly one picture caught her attention. It was a painting of a huge grey horse with a tiny ballerina sitting sideways on its back, her skirt flying up, and a ringmaster cracking his whip. Bon read the title: *Equestrienne (At the Circus Fernando)*.

Big Idea

When Sam came to Peppermint Plain the next day, Bonnie showed her the picture. 'Doesn't it look fantastic? I reckon we could do something like that for the Talent Night. I wonder how we can find out more about it?'

'Let's Google it on your dad's computer,' said Sam. 'Put in "trick-riding horses" and see what we get.'

The girls followed links to find photos of people stepping from one horse to another, galloping 'Roman style' on two horses, leaping through fire, and doing the 'suicide drag' – hanging head-down between the horse's back legs.

Sam loved the stories about 'Poodles' Hanneford, who was famous in the olden days for somersaulting off the back of one horse onto another one following behind.

'Imagine that.' She peered into the screen. 'It
says he was a clown, too. He used to pretend to
almost fall off all the time.'

Bonnie liked the sound of Rebel Watts.
They found pictures of her leaping around her
galloping horses like a sequinned fairy.

'It looks so cool. Let's go and practise,'
she said.

The hayshed was the perfect place. They pulled hay bales down from the stack and used them as horses. Bonnie was as nimble as a flea. She could do a somersault in the air. Sam was the opposite.

'You're a POG,' said Bonnie, as she tried to help her friend roll forwards. 'A Prisoner Of Gravity. But your balance is good. We can be a team.'

It wasn't long before Bon could do a backwards somersault off one hay bale onto another, with Sam standing steady to catch her. They had plenty of bruises and scrapes for their efforts.

'That goes with the territory,' said Bon. 'Rebel broke thirty-seven bones during her career.'

'You're pretty good on the flat,' said Sam, when they stopped for a breather. 'But you need to have a go on something that moves. What about Pedro?'

Bonnie's dad Chester had been bitten by a horse when he was a little boy, and he vowed then that when Peppermint Plain was his it would be horse-free. But he loved cattle, and Peppermint Plain Pedro was his favourite Hereford bull.

Pedro was in the yard beside the hayshed. He was as quiet as an old dog, and let Sam catch him with a piece of baling twine.

PEDRO

Pedro didn't mind when Bonnie vaulted onto his back and stood up straight. She gripped his curly coat with her toes.

'Maybe it's easier on a bull than a horse, Sam. His back is very flat.' She swayed as Sam led Pedro into a walk, but kept her balance. He rolled from side to side, his old hooves creaking. 'Okay, Sam, I'm going to try a somersault.' Bonnie flipped into the air and Sam thought it looked good, but then Pedro exploded into a buck. Bonnie landed on top of Sam and they fell in a heap.

'I think we need a horse,' said Bonnie.

The Perfect Pony

The girls had ridden all the horses and ponies of Currawong Creek at some time. Now they made a list, to work out which one would be the best for trick riding.

Drover, Sam's dad's horse, was their favourite. They double-dinked everywhere on her when she wasn't doing police work, but she was too big.

'Let's face it,' said Sam, 'we're going to fall off a lot, so the less distance we have to fall, the better.'

Too tall   Too nervous   Too ugly!

Tarzan was too grumpy. Bonnie's first pony Bella was too small. Her paddock mate Whale was way too big. Horrie the racehorse was too nervous. 'And too skinny,' said Sam. 'It would hurt your feet to stand on his bony back.'

Chocolate Charme the dressage horse was a bit tall, and anyway Cheryl Smythe-Tyght only let the girls ride Chocko under her strict supervision.

Blondie the palomino was moody and unpredictable, and Tex the Appaloosa was just too ugly.

Too moody   Way too big   Too grumpy

That left Tricky. Bonnie and Sam looked at each other. Tricky would be perfect.

'What about Michael?' said Sam. 'He might say no, just to be a meanie.'

But – surprise, surprise – at school on Monday, Michael said yes.

'Tell me again what you're going to do,' he said, swinging back on his chair with his arms crossed.

Sam took a deep breath. Sometimes Michael was so smug she wanted to punch him in the head.

Bon explained again about the Talent Night, and the trick riding.

'Sure, you can use him.' Michael smiled at
the girls as though he was the Pope. 'But you
and my stupid horse won't stand a chance.
I'm going to win the Talent Night again with
my violin, just like I did last year.'

Learning the Craft

'Tricky's back is nearly as flat as Pedro's,' Bon said as they double-dinked along Currawong Creek, looking for a sandy flat to practise on.

'Mmmn.' Sam couldn't forget Michael's smirk when they told him their plan. 'I hope he doesn't buck you off.'

But Tricky was perfect. With Bonnie on his back he trotted in a circle, keeping an even rhythm and avoiding any small dips in the sand.

'It's as though he wants to make it easy for you,' Sam called from the centre of the circle.

'That's what it feels like.' Bonnie balanced carefully, arms held wide, and smiled into the evening sun. 'He's loving it.'

After a little while, Sam unclipped the long rein from Tricky's headstall and let the pony trot freely. He continued his perfect circles. Bonnie began to experiment, first bending backwards until her hands were resting on Tricky's rump, then kicking up to hold a handstand for a few seconds, then somersaulting onto the ground behind him.

'Woo hoo!' Sam ran over to help her friend up. 'You're a natural, Bon.'

Every afternoon
after school,
Bonnie and Sam
took Tricky down
to Currawong Creek and practised their trick
riding. Bonnie was the star now, and she loved
it. Usually Sam was the best at riding.

Bonnie quickly learned how to use the pony's
rhythm to vault on and off his back while he
trotted, and she could catch a beach ball Sam
threw to her at the same time. She taught Sam
how to swing up too. They developed that
into an act where Bonnie climbed onto Sam's
shoulders and stood, arms outstretched, as
Tricky cantered around and around.

By Friday afternoon they had perfected enough tricks for a ten-minute performance, the maximum time allowed at the Talent Night. They had paid the fifteen-dollar fee and filled in the entry form. They were ready for Saturday night!

Sam sat on a log and watched Bonnie stand on her hands as Tricky trotted past the creek. Evening shadows made stripes across the clearing, flashing light and dark across Tricky's back. Pants ran behind him, yipping in time to his trot.

We're going to win this, Sam thought, imagining herself dressed in the ringmaster costume from the dress-up box, and Bonnie in her tutu. Perhaps Pants could be part of the show too, with a ruffle around her collar.

Broken Dreams

Sam broke out of her daydream when Michael Milton plonked down beside her.

'Great stuff. Really impressive.'

Sam could hardly believe her ears. 'Thanks, Michael. He's an excellent pony.'

'Yes, it's a pity you've gone to all this trouble for nothing.' Michael smirked his nastiest grin, yawned extravagantly and stretched his legs. 'Such a shame they're not allowing any animal acts this year. No exceptions. After the poo problem last year, the hall committee made it a condition.'

'But we can do it outside,' Sam stammered. 'And they've taken our entry money.'

'No,' said Michael. 'They won't let you perform. I heard Mother talking on the phone.' He stood up and yawned again. 'Anyway, I'd better go and practise my violin. She'll kill me if I don't win again.'

As he scuttled away through the shadows, Sam looked across at her clever friend, balancing on Tricky like a bird. He knew all along, she thought. The stinker knew they wouldn't be allowed to perform. That's why he'd been smirking when he said they could use Tricky.

'Bonnie!' she shouted. 'Stop! I've got to tell you something.'

It was true. When the girls asked Stumpy
Shelton, captain of the fire brigade, he said
Michael was right and gave them their money
back. 'I'm sorry, girls, but it's the insurance.
The ruddy insurance.'

Sam could feel tears welling up in her
eyes. Bonnie looked as though she might start
howling too, so Sam put her arm around her.
'Thanks anyway, Mr Shelton,' she mumbled.
'I know it's not your fault.'

Bonnie's mum, Woo, was always willing to fight stupid official decisions, but even she could see that arguing wouldn't do any good this time.

'Let's boycott the Talent Night,' she suggested. 'If they won't let my girls perform, I don't want to go.'

'Thanks, Mum,' said Bonnie. 'But I don't want to be a bad sport. And it was really funny last year, wasn't it, Sam? Even if Michael was a pain.'

'Here's an idea,' said Woo. 'Let's go to the talent show tomorrow, then on Sunday evening we can have a picnic down on the creek, with a special performance of your act, just for our families.'

Bonnie jumped up with a whoop. 'Good on you, Mum! That would be fantastic.'

Sam didn't feel sad any more. 'Come on, Bon. Let's get our costumes organised.' As long as they could perform for the people who loved them, that was all that mattered.

Top Talent

Everybody at the Talent Night had heard about Bonnie and Sam's disappointment. The girls lost count of how many people wished them well.

'It's like we're heroes or something,' Sam murmured to Bonnie.

'That's because we came,' said Bon. 'If we'd stayed away, we'd have looked like sooks.'

Michael played his violin perfectly, and for a while it looked as though he would win.

'It wouldn't be fair if he had two video cameras,' Bon whispered, and Sam felt a nasty stab of jealousy.

But the last act of the night stole the show. Shy Mr Briggs the butcher and his little girl Tamsin sang 'You Are My Sunshine' together, dancing and holding up cardboard shapes of sunshine, clouds and rain. They were so sweet that the applause lasted nearly five minutes, making them clear winners.

The Morgan family came second with their version of 'Do-Re-Mi' from *The Sound of Music*. Mrs Morgan had sewn costumes for them out of curtain material, and the audience clapped for her hard work as much as her family's terrible singing.

Michael came third, and he wasn't happy. 'What good is free photo processing when I haven't got a camera?' Bonnie overheard him grumbling. 'You'll have to buy me one, Mother.'

the Circus Comes to Town

Thunderclouds rolled in on Sunday, so
the picnic and trick-riding show had to be
postponed until the next weekend. By Monday,
the sun was out again and the whole town
looked washed clean.

When Bonnie and Sam checked the horses,
as usual, on the way home from school, they
heard a loud hammering coming from the footy
ground. An enormous tent was going up.

'It's the circus! I'd forgotten all about it!'
Bonnie pulled Sam's arm and started running.
'Let's check it out.'

Caravans and trucks were parked around the
edge of the oval with the big tent in the middle.
The girls squeezed between two vans and
stared at the busy scene. There was so much
going on that nobody noticed them. People
were hammering in huge tent pegs, putting up
temporary yards, attaching annexes to caravans.
Everyone was running.

Bonnie read aloud some of the advertising
painted on the vans. 'Old Macdonald's Clever
Cows; The Flying Pans; Cisco the Clown; Samson,
the Biggest Horse in Australia; Doctor Dog
and his Tailwaggers; Bomberino the Fire-eater;
Miguel's Performing Horses and La Bella Donna,
the Trick Rider.' Bonnie gave a little squeal. 'It's
gonna be fantastic! Lets go and find the horses.'

Circus Horses

'What are you kids doing?' A skinny man in a black cowboy hat appeared in front of them. 'You can't just wander around here.'

Sam stood her ground. 'Anyone can be here. It's the footy oval.'

The man smiled and smoothed his thin moustache. 'Pardon me, señoritas.' He pulled a folded paper from the back pocket of his dirty jeans, and waved it in the air. 'This permit from the council says we can use this ground exclusively for the next week. Circo's Circus, which means me, Mr Circo, can tell anybody to get out.' He pushed the paper under Sam's nose and bowed. 'And I am telling you to get out. Vamoose! On your way, ladies. Come back on Friday night for the show.'

Bonnie and Sam headed for the main gate, walking backwards sometimes to see as much as they could. Mr Circo watched them all the way.

'He's making sure we don't duck around behind a truck,' said Sam, waving to him. 'But I know how to get in the back of the grandstand. We can hide up high and watch from there.'

The girls sat together on the very top step of the grandstand. It was perfect. They could see the whole arena with all the horses. Trucks and caravans were parked all around, to screen it from the road.

'Wow! That horse is as big as a house,' Bon pointed. 'He'd make Whale look like a pony. It must be Samson.'

They watched a slim figure lead a black pony into the arena and start to lunge him in a circle.

'That must be Bella Donna.' Sam squinted to see the girl's face. 'She doesn't look much older than us.'

Now the pony was circling smoothly. The girl unclipped the lunging rein, ran beside him and vaulted onto his back.

'Look! She's got a special saddle thing, Bonnie. That would make it so much easier. There's a handle on the pommel and loops for your feet.'

Bonnie couldn't take her eyes off the rider. 'I'd love to talk to her, but they don't seem very friendly.'

Circus Girl

On Tuesday after school, Bonnie and Sam took Tricky down to the creek again.

'The Talent Night's over, losers,' sneered Michael. 'Why are you still practising?'

The girls just ignored him. Bonnie had taught Pants how to run in front of Tricky, holding his lead rein. They wanted to see if Tricky would run in circles after Pants without the rein.

Sam put an old pony pad on Tricky, with a breastplate, and it made things much easier for Bonnie. She was trying to do the suicide drag, lying right back on Tricky's rump, when he snorted and pulled up suddenly.

'What the...?' Bonnie sat up and her heart jumped. On the other side of the creek was the girl from the circus, on her black pony. Her reins were loose and the pony seemed to be waiting for a signal.

'Come over!' Bonnie shouted. 'It's not deep.'

The black pony picked his way across
Currawong Creek as delicately as a ballet dancer,
and the girl sat on his back like a princess.

Bonnie slid off Tricky and stepped forward.

'Hi, you must be Bella Donna. I'm Bonnie,'
she said.

Sam poked a finger to her chest. 'And I'm Sam.'

The beautiful dark-eyed girl smiled. 'Actually, I'm just Bella, Bella Salvador. The Donna part is just for show.' She slid off her gleaming pony and patted his neck. 'And this is Jet. What about you two? You look like you're trick riders too.'

'Not proper trick riders,' Bon said. 'We're just learning.'

She jumped aside as Tricky barged up to Jet, ears pricked, and the two ponies sniffed each other. The tension broke with a squeal and a toss of heads.

Sam pulled Tricky away. 'Sorry. He has terrible manners. He thinks he's the star.'

'He could be,' Bella said. 'He's beautiful.'

Bonnie and Sam told her about the Talent Night and their squashed dreams.

'Yesterday, we saw your special saddle, so we were experimenting with Sam's old pony pad,' Bonnie explained. 'Until now I've been doing it all bareback.'

Bella ran her hand along Tricky's back. 'I couldn't do what you've been doing, bareback. But I can show you some of my tricks.'

The next two hours went faster than any time Bonnie had ever known, as Bella shared her skills. When it was time to go, Sam invited Bella to her house after school the next day. 'We'll meet here at four o'clock, okay?'

More About the Circus

Next day, everybody was talking about the circus.

'They don't even have lions and elephants,' scoffed Michael Milton.

Bonnie and Sam didn't tell a soul about meeting Bella Donna, but they defended the circus fiercely.

'It's cruel to make wild animals perform,' Bonnie told the class, 'so they use domestic animals, like cows and dogs and horses.'

CIRCO'S CIRCUS

⭐ Old MacDonald's CLEVER COWS !!
⭐ the FLYING PANS !
⭐ CISCO the CLOWN !!
⭐ SAMPSON, the BIGGEST HORSE in AUSTRALIA !!
⭐ DOCTOR DOG & his TAILWAGGERS !!
⭐ BELLA DONNA, the TRICK RIDER !!
⭐ BOMBERINO, the FIRE EATER !!
⭐ MIGUEL's PERFORMING HORSES !!

CURRAWONG CREEK FOOTBALL OVAL
THIS WEEK ONLY!

Bella arrived after school, and the three girls talked for hours about their different lives. It turned out that Bella's family lived on a farm in Queensland when the circus wasn't touring.

'Nanna and Pop look after things while we're away,' she said.

Bella had twin six-year-old brothers who dressed up as baby pandas in the circus. 'Everybody has something to do,' she explained. 'Even when I was a baby, Dad made me part of the show. That's how it is in a circus.'

'My dad told me that when he was little the circus kids used to go to Currawong Creek school while they were in town,' said Sam.

'Yep, that's right,' Bella nodded. 'My dad hated it.' She rubbed Pants's tummy with her foot. 'Our mums and dads had a rotten time, always changing schools. So now we have our own travelling school, with a teacher and a special caravan. And we do correspondence work on the internet.'

The Accident

When Bella came to the creek on Thursday, she
had put the trick-riding saddle on Jet, so she
could show the girls her fancy tricks.

Jet's glossy coat shimmered as he circled
neatly, neck arched. When Bella finished her
full routine, Bonnie and Sam clapped and
hooted like lunatics.

'Okay.' Bella swung off her pony. 'Now it's your turn.'

It was as though Tricky wanted to impress Jet. He didn't put a foot wrong, and Bonnie danced on his back like a fairy. Bella couldn't get over how well Bonnie balanced bareback.

Then Bella sat on Tricky, and he trotted forward. 'Whoo! He feels so different from Jet!' she called, and jumped to her feet in one fluid movement. But, that very moment, Tricky stumbled on a patch of heavy sand and sent Bella flying through the air. She looked so graceful that Bonnie and Sam started to clap, but the scream she let out as she hit the ground silenced them.

'Oooh! My ankle!' she cried, holding her foot. 'I think it's broken!' She huddled over, making squeaky crying noises.

'Let me see.' Sam patted
Bella's shoulder.

'I must have landed
on something hard. Sorry.
I never cry. Really.
But this hurts.'

Bella's ankle was as fat as a piglet.

'It needs ice,' Sam said. 'I'll race up to the
house and get some.'

'Mum and Dad will be furious,' Bella sniffed as
Bonnie held a packet of frozen peas against her
ankle. 'My act is always the finale. Mr C. will
probably give Dad the sack if I can't do it.'

'Is your dad Miguel?' Sam asked, still puffing
from her run.

'Yep, Miguel's Performing Horses,' Bella
replied. 'But he hurt his back last year and
hasn't been able to ride since. Mr Circo has
been threatening to get a new horse master for
months. If it wasn't for me and the twins, he
would have.'

'I thought he looked like a rat,' said Sam. 'Let me bandage your ankle. I don't think it's broken, just badly sprained.' Sam knew a lot about First Aid from her dad.

'What am I going to do?' wailed Bella. 'I can't even stand up. There's no way it's going to be better by tomorrow night.'

'Maybe Bonnie can fill in for you,' Sam suggested.

'That's it!' For the first time since her fall, Bella smiled. 'You could easily do it, Bonnie. Look at us, we're nearly the same size and shape. With my costume and make-up on, nobody will be able to tell the difference.'

Bonnie felt a shiver of excitement. A real circus rider!

'Come on,' Bella begged her. 'Please say you'll at least try. Hop on Jet now and see how you go.'

But when Bonnie hopped on Jet, he wouldn't go at all. He laid his ears back flat against his head, so he looked like a black snake, and refused to move.

All the girls' cajoling and bossing made no difference. Even when Bonnie leaned forward and whispered her special horse talk in his ear, Jet wouldn't budge. He only went for one rider, and that was Bella.

'You're a pig, Jet,' Bella shouted at him, crying tears of frustration. 'I hate you!'

'I saw a horse do this at the Melbourne Cup one year,' Sam said, trying to calm Bella. 'I was watching it on TV and this horse just stopped on the way to the starting stalls and wouldn't budge for anyone. You can't make a horse do something it doesn't want to do.'

'I bet it didn't get much dinner that night,' Bon laughed, and then added, as a joke, 'I could always do the performance on Tricky. If we painted his legs black and put a big saddlecloth on him to cover his white bits, most people wouldn't know the difference.'

Bella shook both fists in the air. 'You're a genius, Bonnie,' she shouted. 'Put my saddle on Tricky right away and I'll teach you my routine.'

Bonnie wasn't nearly as slick as Bella, but she could do everything except the grand finale. She was supposed to do a somersault in the air and land on Tricky's back.

Tricky had to slow down at exactly the right time, but after getting so good at trotting steadily he didn't want to slow down. Each time, Bonnie landed on the ground instead of on his back.

'It will just have to do,' Bella said. 'Most people will think that's what's supposed to happen anyway.'

Bonnie and Sam helped her onto Jet's back, then swung onto Tricky.

'What about your mum?' Bonnie asked. 'She's got to notice you can't walk.'

Bella shifted in the saddle. 'Tonight I'll pretend I have only one leg.'

Sam smiled. It was the kind of crazy thing she and Bonnie would do. Her dad would just roll his eyes and say, 'What next?'

'Then tomorrow I'll ask Mum if I can have my day in bed. She lets us have one day in bed each term.'

Mrs Salvador sounded like a very cool mum.

'I'll have to tell the twins. They love secrets. I'll tell them to bring Jet to your house at six o'clock. I'll disappear, so Mum thinks I'm getting ready. You can swap Tricky for Jet and come back with the boys.'

'Mighty fine plan,' Sam laughed. 'I'll put Jet in the paddock with Drover.'

The three girls smacked hands in a high five, then turned their horses towards home.

Secrets

'What do you think?' Sam held up a crimson satin tablecloth with aqua tassels and 'Greetings from Hervey Bay' printed in one corner. 'This should cover most of Tricky's white bits.'

'Cool', said Bon. 'Help me black out the rest.'

The girls brushed Tricky until he shone and plaited his mane and tail.

Then Sam painted Bon's face in the way Bella had suggested: white with red cheeks, like a marionette.

When Bella's brothers came through the garden they were so alike that the girls couldn't help laughing. They were tiny, with short black hair and big brown eyes.

'They look like pandas even without their costumes,' Sam whispered.

'Hi, boys. I'm Sam and this is Bonnie. She's going to fill in for Bella tonight.'

Alphonso and Augustin were extremely serious about the operation. One of them handed Bonnie a bulging plastic bag. 'This is her costume. She said to make sure you put the tights on first or it won't work.'

'We've got to go on at seven-fifteen, so you have to hurry,' said the other.

Sam draped the tablecloth over Tricky's back, and lowered Bella's trick-riding saddle onto it.

'Make sure you do the girth up tight,' said Alphonso or Augustin, 'or she'll come a gutser.'

Under the Big Top

Sam sat between her dad and Bon's parents, watching the little boys in their panda suits. They teased the clown and ringmaster, pushing them from behind, then hid behind barrels and balls. The crowd roared with laughter.

'Where's Bon?' Woo asked again. 'It's not like her to miss the action.'

'She's helping Bella. You know, the circus girl we met.' Sam's face went red whenever she told a fib, so she was glad the lights were dim.

They watched the Flying Pans whizz through the air above them, laughed until they wept at the clever cows and dogs, shrieked in fear for Bomberino the Fire-eater, and gasped at Samson, the Biggest Horse in Australia.

Sam could see that Bella's father had a sore back by the way he walked, but he still looked dignified. The horses watched him all the time,

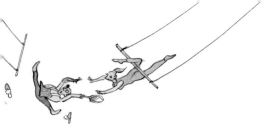

as though they were determined to do their very best. Sam's dad noticed it too.

'He's a real horseman,' he nudged Sam. 'See how the horses love him.'

They clapped until their hands were sore when ten tiny ponies trotted nose to tail underneath the giant Samson, who nodded his head as each one passed.

'Thank you, ladies and gentlemens, girls and boys!' Mr Circo shouted, as Miguel and his horses left the big top. 'And now for our final act, our world-class equestrienne, La Bella Donna!'

The Big Moment

Sam felt sick as Tricky entered the arena with Bonnie sitting bravely on his back. He looked frightened, ready to shy at anything. What if he wouldn't go? But Bon leaned forward, whispered in his ear, and his expression changed.

Music filled the tent, and Tricky began to circle over the sawdust. Bonnie sat still at first, arms stretched wide, and the audience hushed.

She looks like the real deal, thought Sam.

Mr Circo didn't seem to have noticed anything wrong. He was standing alone in the middle of the ring, watching the audience.

Suddenly Bonnie jumped to her feet and began bouncing from Tricky onto the ground and up again, standing on her hands, spinning, twisting and hanging her head between his back legs. Her movements were so quick in the glittering golden costume that it was hard to believe a human could move so lightly and so fast.

Tricky was perfect, his neck arched, his black legs criss-crossing neatly over the sawdust. Bonnie spun above him like a golden fairy, working through Bella's tricks.

As she slowed for the finale, Mr Circo boomed into the microphone. 'And now, La Bella Donna will zomersault and land once more on ze pony's back.'

The music softened and he lowered his voice dramatically. 'I remind you, ladies and gentlemens, that ze zomersault takes time, and in zat time ze pony moves. Ozer riders 'ave zomersaulted onto anozer 'orse, ozer riders have zomersaulted onto ze ground, but none but La Bella Donna has zomersaulted onto ze same 'orse. It takes a great understanding between 'orse and rider to achieve zis feat! Ladies and gentlemens, I present ze Zuper Zomersault!'

Sam held her breath. What was Bonnie going to do? Everyone was waiting for a trick she'd never managed before.

Bonnie leaned forward again to whisper in Tricky's ear, and the crowd murmured. It seemed as if the pony was listening to her. But when she flung herself into the air, it was clear that he hadn't slowed enough for her to land properly. She landed way back on his rump, slipped, twisted, then hung back with her head between Tricky's hind legs in a suicide drag.

The crowd gasped then applauded as Bonnie pulled herself back onto the pony. Almost immediately she fell sideways, and Sam screamed, like the rest of the audience.

As Bonnie turned that near-fall into another move, Sam realised she was playing the clown, like Poodles Hanneford. If she couldn't do the somersault, she was going to give them a laugh. But when Sam looked at Mr Circo's face, he wasn't laughing.

The Rescue

Sam squeezed past Woo who was too mesmerised by La Bella Donna to notice. She hurried out of the tent and stood in the dark, whistling, the same long whistle, over and over. Laughter and applause from inside the big top told her that Bon was still clowning.

Suddenly a white shape rushed out of the dark. 'Pants!' She hugged her dog and got a wet lick in return. 'You little beauty!'

Sam and Pants wriggled under the seats to the front row. 'Pants, I need you to slow Tricky down. Here, you scruffy girl,' she said, pulling the lime-green scrunchy out of her hair and putting it around Pants's neck. 'Now you look like a circus dog.' She kissed Pants on the nose, then put her down. 'Go Pants! Lead Tricky!'

The crowd roared even louder when the little dog entered the ring and ran proudly in front of

Tricky. Tricky slowed to follow Pants. Mr Circo
looked as though he was going to explode.

Bon saw Pants, too, and knew this was her
only chance. She gathered her strength, and
then twisted up and backwards, spinning,
spinning... and landed on Tricky's back.

The crowd went crazy. Bonnie had done the
Super Somersault. She stood up straight, arms
held high, as Tricky cantered around the ring,
with wave after wave of applause washing over
her golden sequinned suit.

Found Out

When Sam burst into the dressing tent, all she could see in the glare was Bonnie, Bella and Tricky. 'You did it!' she screamed. 'You were fantastic! Nobody could tell the difference!'

'I could tell the difference.' Suddenly Sam realised that Bella's parents were there. Mrs Salvador was tiny and dark, like Bella. 'I knew straight away that it wasn't my daughter,' she said.

'And I knew it was *my* daughter,' said a voice behind them. Woo pushed past Sam, followed by Bon's dad, and Bill Cooper. 'I think you kids better tell us what's going on.'

After that it turned into a party. The adults were secretly proud of their clever kids.

Mr Circo didn't know whether to shout with anger or happiness. 'And what if your friend hadn't been a natural rider?' he asked Bella. 'What then?' He smoothed his moustache, sighed loudly and looked upwards. 'You must never go riding on ponies again. You're too important for the circus. Understand?'

He ruffled Bella's hair and hugged Mrs Salvador. 'But maybe, Miguel,' he said to Bella's dad, 'maybe we will have to work some of Bonnie's clown act into the show.'

The Real Finale

On Saturday, there was a picnic at Bonnie and
Sam's practice spot beside Currawong Creek.
Aunty Birdy came, and Janice and Bob from the
newsagency, and Cheryl Smythe-Tyght. Bella's
parents and little brothers and Mr Circo and
some other circus families were there too.

Tricky was black-and-white again. Pants ran
in front of Tricky with a purple ruffle around
her neck, looking very important.

Bonnie and Sam started their performance
with simple tricks, and the applause got louder
after each move. When Bonnie finally stood
on Sam's shoulders and double-somersaulted
backwards onto the ground, everyone went
crazy. Even Mr Circo was impressed.

As the sky turned pink then faded to purple,
the families sat on rugs in the sandy clearing
and shared a feast. Sam's dad and Miguel

chatted over the barbeque sausages, and realised they had sat together in school, thirty years ago.

'I never forgot you,' said Miguel. 'You helped me with long division.'

Next day, as the circus was leaving, Bonnie and Sam rode beside Bella's caravan to the outskirts of town, double-dinking on Tricky.

'She'll always be our friend,' said Bonnie as the circus cavalcade disappeared down the road. 'Won't she?'

'That's right,' said Sam, kicking Tricky into a canter. 'We are the Tricky Trio. The girls who tricked a town.'

The girls put Tricky back in his paddock, and rewarded him with carrots for his good work. Michael Milton raced up and skidded to a stop on his new mountain bike.

'Did ya go to the circus?' He sat back and spun his front wheel. 'That Bella Donna on Jet was fantastic. Not like you and my stupid horse.'

Bonnie and Sam laughed so hard that they fell over.

Tricky raced around the paddock, bucking and farting, and Pants ran after him, barking.

'What's so funny?' asked Michael.

BONNIE and SAM
Racing the Tide

For Holly A.L.
For Oppy R.H.

Christmas is over

Bonnie and Sam knew all the horses and ponies
in Currawong Creek. They were **horse-crazy!**

Christmas had come and gone, and again
neither of the girls got the horse they wanted
from Santa. Sam and her dad, Bill, spent
Christmas Day in the city with her cousins.
Bonnie's parents, Chester and Woo, hosted

a huge family lunch at Peppermint Plain. Now all that was left was the decorations.

Sam stared up at the beautiful Christmas tree in Bonnie's lounge room. Woo was an artist and she always made crazy Christmas trees. This year she had filled an old tank with dead eucalypt branches, sprayed them silver and gold and hung red paper cranes from them.

'I made three and Chester made one, but Mum made all the rest,' Bonnie said proudly.

Holidays!

Now that Sam was back from the city, the holidays could begin. It was a delicious feeling having all of January just for fun, and to make it even better, the girls had horses to ride too.

Sam's father was the local policeman and he always let the girls ride his mare, Drover, when he didn't need her for police work. The girls shared a secret about Drover and loved double-dinking on her, but having a horse each was even better.

Janice and Bob, who ran the newsagency, were going away for a weeks holiday and had asked Bonnie and Sam to take care of their horses. The girls had spent the last weeks of school planning their horsey holiday. Of all the horses in Currawong Creek, Blondie and Tex were two of their favourites. Blondie was a beautiful palomino quarter horse, who could

sometimes be moody. Tex was an appaloosa
with a pink nose. He had the sweetest nature a
horse could have. Nothing shocked Tex.

'Who do you want to ride?' Sam asked,
looking at the map of Wild Dog Hills.

'I don't mind.' Bonnie traced Currawong Creek
with her finger. 'Let's see how it works out.
Where will we go first?'

'I'm sorry to spoil your plans, girls.' Woo looked embarrassed. 'I forgot to tell you, Bonnie. Violet and Woody asked if you'd help them with shearing next week and I said you would. I didn't know you and Sam had plans.'

'How could you, Mum?' Bonnie rolled her eyes. 'We always have plans!'

If she and Sam didn't have Blondie and Tex for the week, Bonnie would have loved the thought of helping out Aunty Vi and Uncle Woody. Their farm, Banksia Ridge, was right on the coast, and the bush and beach were full of surprises.

Bonnie's dad, Chester, had two older sisters: Aunty Birdy, who knew everything about horses, and Aunty Violet, who knew everything about sheep. They both thought Bonnie was the best thing since sliced bread.

'Maybe Sam can go with you. You two would have a fabulous time,' said Woo.

'We've promised Janice and Bob, though,' said Bonnie. 'Can't we go and help them *after* we look after Blondie and Tex? That way we can do both things.'

'No.' Woo shook her head. 'They have to shear next week. The shearing team is booked in. They go to the same farms at the same time every year.'

'Why do they have to do it now?' Bon was like a dog with a bone when she argued. 'Why organise it for the middle of the holidays?'

'It actually makes sense, Bonnie. The lambs have all been sold, so they don't have to put them through the yards. And it's getting hot. It's the perfect time for the ewes to have their woolly coats removed. There's nothing more to say. I promised them you'd help and that's what you're going to do.'

Making plans

'We've got two days to ride before you have to go.' Sam was trying to cheer Bonnie up as they waited for Janice at the newsagency. Bonnie was flipping through a copy of *Horse Deals*. She loved looking at all the beautiful horses for sale.

'Look at this pinto that's been stolen.' Bonnie opened the page for Sam to see. 'He looks like a black and white version of Bella.'

'Hi girls!' Janice came from the back of the shop with a stack of newspapers. 'How are my horse-sitters this morning?' Janice was dressed like a cowgirl, as usual, with sequinned horse shoes on her shirt and a big silver belt-buckle.

'It's not good, Janice. Bon has to go and help her aunty and uncle with the shearing the day after tomorrow. I'll still be able to look after Blondie and Tex, but we were really looking forward to riding up in the mountains together.'

'Where's their farm?' Janice turned to get another pile of papers. She was always on the move. If you wanted to talk to her you had to go with her.

'Out on the coast,' Bonnie called after her. 'Out at Whale Bay.'

Bonnie and Sam pushed past the photocopier and the card rack to the kitchen at the back of the shop.

'Whale Bay is only about thirty kilometres away,' Janice said over a cup of tea. 'You could ride out.' Bonnie and Sam stared in stunned silence at Janice's good idea.

'You should both go and help with shearing and take Blondie and Tex with you. They'd love it, though Tex doesn't like getting his feet wet. He hates water.' She turned to go. 'Maybe you can persuade him to go for a swim.'

The farrier came the next day to put new shoes on Blondie and Tex for the ride out to Banksia Ridge. The girls loved Clint and he never minded their questions. 'See how I'm bending the tip of the nail a little bit?' Half under Tex, Clint held up the hammer and nail so the girls could see. 'A little bend like this makes sure the nail angles out, not in, where it would hurt. The nails are bevelled anyway, but I like to do an extra bit, just to be sure.'

The paddock behind Janice and Bob's news-agency was like a suntrap. Blondie dozed as she waited for her turn and Tex was half asleep too.

Clint's little dog, Cactus, and Sam's dog, Smartie
Pants, hung around Clint as closely as the girls.
The dogs made happy growling sounds as they
chewed on hoof clippings.

Clint gently put Tex's hoof down and stood
up and stretched his back. 'Whale Bay, hey?'
He took his tools across to Blondie and reached
down for her hoof. 'They reckon there's some
serious abalone poaching going on out there.'

Poachers!

'What are abalone?' Sam had never heard the word.

'They're those big shells, Sam.' Bonnie patted Blondie's neck as Clint began to trim her hoof. 'You know those mother-of-pearl shells that people always use as ashtrays? They have a disgusting slimy thing that lives in them. It's like a sucker, clings to the rocks. You have to dive down and prise them off with a screwdriver.'

'Why would anyone poach them?'

'They're worth a fortune. Some people think they're delicious. They are really yummy, once they're cleaned and cooked. If you have a licence you can take five a day, I think. There's a limit, to protect them, so they don't become extinct. Woo dives for them sometimes at the Cape but I've never been game to. You have to go down through the kelp, and there are big black stingrays there.'

Clint threw a curve of trimmed hoof and Cactus and Pants chased after it. 'Abalone is big business,' he said. 'A commercial licence to get them is worth more than a million dollars and the abalone meat sells for nearly one hundred dollars a kilo. There'll always be a black market for it.' Sam passed him a shoe. 'Your dad will be able to tell you more about it, but word at the pub is that Soggy Stevens is at it again. He's been caught heaps of times, had his boat confiscated and everything, but he's done his time and now he's got another boat. He takes the boat down to Whale Bay every day and dives – says he's doing research, as if. The police know he's diving for abs but they can't catch him with any in the boat. It's a mystery.'

That evening Sam asked her father about
Soggy Stevens.

'Soggy's been to jail and fined more
times than I can remember and he still won't
stop. He's addicted to diving for abalone,'
Bill said, shaking his head. 'I'd love to catch
him at it.'

Sam pushed her baked beans around the
plate. Sometimes when Bill was busy with
police work his dinners weren't very exciting.

'Well, maybe Bon and I will find some
evidence while we're at Whale Bay.'

After dinner Sam walked around to visit
Bonnie's Aunty Birdy. She had promised to lend
the girls her saddle bags for their long ride.

'This would be a good place to stop for lunch,'
Aunty Birdy said, finger on the map. 'Platypus
Creek. You'll be able to give the horses a drink
and I think there's even a picnic table there.'

Bonnie would bring the food and drinks
when she came into town tomorrow for their
early start, but Sam still found plenty to prepare:
sunscreen, insect repellent and lollies. She
packed her bag, too, for the weeks stay. It felt
good to be on the brink of an adventure.

setting out

'Good luck! Look out for cars!' Aunty Birdy had
helped the girls saddle up, and now she waved
them on their way.

'I'll see you there when I bring your bags out!'
Bill called.

Sam rode Blondie and Bonnie rode Tex. They felt like cowgirls riding through the main street of Currawong Creek. It was so early the shops were still shut.

'It's like in a movie, when the baddies ride into town and everybody goes inside,' joked Bonnie.

'Yeah,' said Sam. '*Yee har!* Let's go!' The horses broke into an eager canter and, with Pants at their heels, clattered up the deserted street and out onto the coast road.

It was a still, sunny day and the old dirt road to the coast was quiet. If a car did come the girls would hear it from a long way away and get onto the verge. They rode through open farm land where white-faced cattle stared at them in silence and magpies perched in lines on gates, carolling as they passed.

Sometimes the road wound through the bush and dappled shade made the morning air cool.  A kookaburra swooped past them, and on one straight stretch a lyrebird scurried across the road, his lacy tail trailing behind.

It took all morning to get to Platypus Creek.

'This must be it, Sam.' Bonnie looked down at a small grassy flat, where a creek gurgled around one side and tall gum trees made patches of shade. They rode the horses down the gentle bank to water them at the creek. Blondie waded right in, so the water was just below her belly, but Tex stayed at the edge. No matter how sweetly Bonnie whispered to him in horse-talk 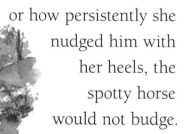 or how persistently she nudged him with her heels, the spotty horse would not budge.

'I don't think we'll be going swimming at Whale Bay,' Sam said.

Woo had made corned beef sandwiches for lunch. Bonnie whistled Pants so she could feed her the crusts but Pants took a long time to come to the picnic table.

'What's she got in her mouth?' Sam put her sandwich down. 'Come here.' Pants presented her find. 'Pooh! It stinks!' She took a closer look. 'Hey, Bonnie, it's one of those shells!' It was an abalone shell, with some abalone meat still inside it.

'That's only been dumped a couple of days ago, Sam.' Bonnie had her detective face on. 'And what's it doing here, so far from the sea?'

'Show us, Pants,' Sam urged the little dog. 'Show us where you got it.'

They followed her along the creek a short way, and there, behind a patch of ti-tree, was a big pile of silver shells.

'It's got to be poachers, Sam.' Bonnie's eyes were huge. 'There must be a hundred shells here.'

Banksia Ridge

The girls saw the sea for the first time as they
rode up from Platypus Creek, then spent all
afternoon getting closer to it. When they crested
the last big hill they could see paddocks stretched
out behind Whale Bay and the house and sheds,
sheltered by the ridge of banksias that gave the
farm its name. The road was a sand track now
and the horses' hooves were soft upon it.

Six sheepdogs raced out barking as the girls approached the sheds, bearing down on Pants like a gang of bullies and sniffing her all over.

A piercing whistle sent them all flying back and a skinny figure appeared, wiping his hands on his trousers.

'That's Uncle Woody,' Bonnie told Sam.

The old man turned to the house as he walked towards them. 'Vi!' he bellowed. 'Our drovers are here!'

Sam had never seen such a messy farm. Bonnie's father, Chester, believed in putting things away and Peppermint Plain was as tidy as a park. Here at Banksia Ridge, there was stuff everywhere: old trucks and cars, tractors, rusty farm machines, sheds, yards, and almost hidden by a wild garden, the house, with a sagging red roof.

Vi showed them where to tie the horses while they unsaddled and washed them down. The enormous, leaning shed was full of dusty harness and saddlery, cracked and perished with age.

Vi noticed Sam staring. 'Yes, we used to have a lot of horses out here. My father, Bonnie's grandfather, sowed all this country to pasture using horses. In the olden days, this place and Peppermint Plain were part of the same cattle run.'

Pants barked suddenly, her 'I-hear-Bill's-car' bark, and sure enough, his police four-wheel drive pulled up at the shed.

As Bill carried their bags to the house, Sam told him about the abalone shells at Platypus Creek and he congratulated the girls on their fine detective work.

'There's something strange going on, that's for sure,' sniffed Uncle Woody. 'We've seen some lights at night, down the beach and out at sea.'

'That's right,' said Aunty Vi. 'Down towards Skull Rock.'

Drover girls

The next day Bonnie and Sam worked all
morning mustering sheep and droving them
back to the shearing shed. Aunty Vi rode a
quad bike and Uncle Woody followed behind
in the battered ute. 'Since my hip seized up
it's the only way I can get around,' he explained
to Sam.

The collie dogs skulked around the sheep like spies, cutting off escapees and barking at the slowcoaches. The youngest dog, Barney, kept doing the wrong thing until Vi got sick of yelling and made him sit behind her on the bike.

Bonnie was used to herding cattle and sheep, but Sam had never been a drover before. It took a while to figure out how to make the sheep go the way you wanted them to, but once they took off the mob flowed across the paddock like lava.

By lunch time three hundred sheep were locked in the pens under the shearing shed, ready to be shorn the next day.

'Now it doesn't matter if it rains,' said Vi.

'You can't shear them if they're wet,' Bonnie explained to Sam.

the hut

After lunch Bonnie and Sam followed the track
across the sand dunes to go riding on the beach.
Indigo clouds hung over the horizon, leaking
columns of rain into the sea. The horses snorted
and propped when they saw the wide expanse
of the beach and crashing surf. At the water's
edge Blondie plunged straight in, splashing
through the shallows like a toddler.

'Come on, boy,' Bonnie whispered to Tex.
'It's only water. You'll love it.'

But Tex would not go in. He ducked and
danced and scurried sideways like a crab to
avoid even the tiniest creeping line of foam.

When the girls swapped horses, he was just
as stubborn for Sam, ignoring her drumming
heels like he'd ignored Bonnie's horse talk.

So they gave up and cantered down the beach,
letting the horses race for a little way, then
easing them back to a canter, a trot,
and finally a walk.

'That's Skull Rock.' Bonnie pointed. 'We have
to watch the tide here. If it comes in too far we
won't be able to get back.'

'And look!' Sam was pointing inland. 'There's
a hut.'

They rode up to a small wooden building
nestled in the lee of the dunes. It was weathered
silver and a lopsided tank held rainwater
from the roof. The only door opened on to a
verandah. Through the small windows the girls
could see two beds and a table.

'Wouldn't it be great to come and stay here,'
they said at the same time.

'Of course you can go and stay there.' Aunty
Vi seemed just as excited as Bonnie and Sam.
'You'll have a lovely time at the old shepherds'
hut. Our kids used to go down there when
they were young.'

After dinner they walked out to the beach, Woody leading the way with his torch, to look for phosphorescence.

'We call them glow bugs,' Bonnie told Sam. 'Sometimes we see heaps of them. They slosh in on the waves then fade on the sand.'

Tonight there were no glow bugs, just the moon shining on the dark sea, and a starry sky. When they turned to go home, Sam spotted a dancing light on the sea. 'What's that?' she called out, but it disappeared as soon as she spoke. Suddenly it flickered again.

'That's down at Skull Rock,' said Vi. 'It's that same light we've been seeing for months now.'

'Maybe it's abalone smugglers,' said Sam.

'Maybe it is,' said Vi in a spooky voice. 'Or maybe it's the ghost of Skull Rock.'

Shearing

'You're going to be busier than a dog with two tails,' Woody told the girls at breakfast. And he was right. By seven-thirty the two shearers, Max and Jimmy, had started shearing – tipping the big ewes onto their bottoms and holding them with their legs. They trimmed all the dags or dirty wool off with the first blow of their shears, then stroke by stroke cut off the creamy fleece.

Jimmy's grandson was the rouseabout, picking up the dirty scraps and bagging them, sweeping the floor and flinging the fleeces on to the slatted table for the wool classer to inspect.

Bonnie and Sam brought the sheep up from under the shed to the holding pens and made sure the catching pens were full. The shorn sheep looked naked and skinny without their thick fleece, and it was funny to see them sliding down the chutes to the outside pens.

Bonnie and Sam kept tally of how many sheep each shearer shore in a dog-eared book.

Smartie Pants loved being a sheep dog, barking and diving in now and then to nip. In the shed all the collies wore muzzles so they couldn't bite, but they barked like banshees. If they had to get somewhere in a hurry they ran across the sheeps' backs like tightrope walkers.

When they stopped for morning tea, on the first morning, Sam was exhausted. But that was only the beginning. She and Bonnie did all sorts of jobs. They helped pile the wool into the bale press, gave Woody a hand with the cooking, pushed the sheep into the pens, passed Vi the drenching gun and marking paint, and finally drove the shorn sheep back to their paddocks.

At the end of the second day they sat on the steps of the grand old shed and waved goodbye to the shearers.

'Well done, girls.' Vi put her arms around Bonnie and Sam. 'You've been a wonderful help. We couldn't have done it without you.'

That night, all four of them fell asleep at the dinner table.

overnight adventure

Bonnie and Sam slept in until late the next morning. In the kitchen, Vi had put everything they needed for their stay at the shepherds' hut into extra saddle bags.

'I won't tell you what food I've packed,' she said. 'That way it'll be a surprise for you. The old stove works well but make sure there are no birds' nests in the chimney before you light it.' She held up a mobile phone. 'And I'm putting this in too. Just in case you need to call us.'

They had a big shearer's breakfast of eggs and bacon, added sleeping bags and clothes to the bags, then saddled the horses and set off. The rain clouds had passed and it was a beautiful summer's day with hardly a breath of wind.

When they got to the hut they checked that the bush paddock was safe and secure for the horses, then they settled in. Sam found an old

broom and swept the floor. Bonnie turned the
mattresses over to make sure there was nothing
creepy underneath, then laid their sleeping bags
out. Their food fitted on the shelves above the
table and there were driftwood pegs to hang
their clothes on. They collected wood for the
stove and put their torches on the table, ready
for dark. Then they flopped on the beds and
enjoyed the feeling of having their own house.

'I feel like a swim,' said Bonnie.

Sam jumped up. 'Good idea. Let's take the horses bareback and try again with Tex.'

The sea was like a big turquoise pond and there were no waves in the bay between the hut and Skull Rock. Blondie walked straight into the deep water until she was swimming. Sam held her mane and floated beside her, then lay on her back again as they came back to shore.

'Have a go on Blondie,' she called to Bonnie. 'She loves it.'

Tex still wouldn't go in the water. They stood the horses side by side and crawled across to swap. 'It's a mid-air horse transfer,' Sam said.

Bonnie cantered Blondie back into the sea

then practised her trick-riding skills, standing
on Blondie's back, then diving off with a
somersault.

Sam tried various ways to get Tex into the
water: bossing him, tricking him and begging
him. Pants even started barking at him, but
nothing worked.

'You are an old stupid Tex,' she said,
exasperated. 'If you tried it, you'd love it.'

Vi's surprise dinner was sausages that Bonnie
and Sam cooked on the old stove, then rolled up
in white bread with tomato sauce.

'Mum and Dad would freak out if they knew
we had a fire,' said Bonnie.

'Yes. I think Vi is used to big kids,' said Sam. She peeped in the firebox. 'We'll just make sure it's out before we go to bed.'

Afterwards they made hot chocolate with powdered milk and dipped their biscuits in it. They cleaned their teeth and spat off the edge of the verandah then climbed into their sleeping bags. By torchlight Sam read aloud a story from an old school reader that Vi had put in the saddle bag. It was about a girl and boy who swam their horses out to rescue some people from a shipwreck, more than one hundred years ago. Before Sam finished both Pants and Bonnie were snoring, so she turned off the torch and fell asleep too.

Ghosts!

Bonnie sat up, her heart pounding. Something had woken her.

Pants was sitting up on Sam's bed, hackles up, growling.

'Sam!' Something thumped the outside of the hut. 'Sam!' Bonnie shook her sleeping friend. 'Wake up, Sam! There's something outside.'

When the girls peered out the back window they screamed together. There *was* something there!

Pants barked sharply.

'What is it, Sam?' Bonnie's teeth were chattering. 'It looks like two ghosts.'

Sam peeped out the window again, then leaned forward, staring. She started to laugh.

'What is it, Sam? Why are you laughing?' Bonnie grabbed at Sam's legs.

164

'It's Blondie and Tex,' said Sam. 'I guess they're sheltering from the wind. They *do* look like ghosts.'

When Bonnie looked into the dark she laughed too. The horses were standing, heads down, with their rumps towards the hut.

'They look like ghosts with no heads.' Bon was relieved to have been frightened by something so harmless. 'Maybe they're the headless horsemen of Shepherds' Hut.'

The sound of the sea that had seemed sinister when she was afraid now soothed her. The two girls and their dog drifted into sleep.

In the morning Bonnie woke up with a feeling that she had forgotten something. Something kept niggling at her mind. They had breakfast in bed: bananas, muesli, sultanas and milk in plastic bowls. As she sat there, staring at the door, it suddenly came to her. She thought hard, in case it was just her imagination, but now she could definitely remember.

'Somebody opened the door last night.'

'What?' Sam choked on her muesli.

'That's what woke me. I can remember now. The door opened and a torch shone in the hut.'

'Are you sure you weren't dreaming, Bon?' Sam asked her friend.

'No, I heard footsteps going off the verandah too. Maybe I couldn't remember last night because it would have been too scary.'

'You *must* have been dreaming,' Sam insisted.

Pants whined politely at the door and Bonnie got up to let her out. 'Ooohh!' She gasped, looking out, then reached down to the floor for something and showed it to Sam. 'This isn't a dream,' she said. 'This is a torch and a rope.'

Sam dialled her home number and waited anxiously while the phone rang. The shepherds' hut suddenly felt a long way from anywhere and she was glad they had Vi's mobile.

'Hi, Dad. It's me, Sam,' she said, surprised that tears welled in her eyes at the sound of his voice.

When she explained what had happened, Bill said they should pack up and ride back to Banksia Ridge.

'Just to be on the safe side,' he said. 'There's probably a rational explanation, and whoever it was will be long gone, but I'd feel better if I knew you were out of there. I'll ring Woody and Vi and let them know you'll be back for lunch. Maybe when I come to pick up your bags tomorrow we'll have a look around.'

They rolled up their sleeping bags and swept the floor again.

'The good thing about a tiny house like this is that there's hardly any housework,' said Bonnie, taking one last look.

'Yep,' said Sam. 'It's a lovely hut. I wish the night visitor hadn't spoiled it for us.' She twisted the latch on the door, making sure it was shut properly. 'Let's go and catch the horses.'

More evidence

Bonnie and Sam walked through the bush at the back of the paddock, calling for the horses. The sky was cloudy again and tiny finches flitted through the trees. When they found the horses they used a stump to get on.

'Don't you love riding bareback?' asked Bonnie.

'Yes,' Sam agreed. 'Especially when the horses have their smooth summer coats.'

They rode towards the hut, following the
fence. The horses suddenly propped, staring.

'What's that?' Sam peered through the trees.

'It's a car. A four-wheel drive with a boat
trailer,' Bonnie whispered.

The horses stood quietly while the girls
looked at the car. Nothing moved.

'Let's go a bit closer,' said Bonnie. 'But be
ready to skedaddle if there's anybody there.'

They rode right up to the fence and peered
over it. 'There's nobody here.' Sam felt uneasy.
'They must be out in the boat, I guess. But why
would they be here?'

'It must be the abalone poachers, Sam,' said Bonnie. 'Try to remember the numberplate and we'll phone your dad.'

'I'll scratch it on my reins with a stick,' Sam said, breaking off a small branch. Bonnie read out the number for her, then they kicked the horses into a canter and rode back to the hut.

While Bonnie saddled the horses, Sam rang her father again.

'That's Soggy's car,' said Bill when Sam told him the number. 'I'm leaving Currawong Creek now. I know the track that leads out to Skull Rock and I'll drive out there to make sure I don't miss them.' His voice rose. 'But I want you and Bonnie AWAY from there! Do you hear me, Sam? Don't mess around, just get going.'

The girls were ready in record time, scared now. 'I'm taking these, too,' Bonnie shoved the torch and rope into a saddle bag. 'It's evidence.'

They trotted away from the hut, and it felt good coming onto the wide expanse of the beach, where nobody could sneak up on them.

The sea was different today, rough and noisy.

They saw the tyre marks immediately. They couldn't miss them: a big curve where the car had turned around, then straight into the sea where the boat had been unloaded. Bonnie followed the tracks until Tex danced away from the waves.

'More evidence, Sam,' she yelled above the waves.

Sam looked out to sea, searching for a boat.
She couldn't spot it, even though she peered like
a hawk. The surf was boiling and further out
the waves glittered and danced.

'Maybe they're behind Skull Rock!' she yelled

to Bonnie. She shifted her focus to the rock and
thought she saw something. 'Look, Bonnie!' She
pointed. 'Their boat must have sunk!' Three tiny
figures were clinging to the base of Skull Rock.
'I can hear them calling for help.'

'I thought that was birds,' said Bonnie. 'But
it's screaming.'

Sam could see why the men were screaming.
Skull Rock was as smooth as a skull, and the
base where they were standing was already
underwater.

The tide was coming in and soon there would
be nothing for the men to hold on to.

As the girls watched, a huge wave sloshed against the rock and knocked the figures down.

'They're going to drown, Bonnie,' said Sam.

So many thoughts raced through Sam's mind that it felt like a big railway station. She dug into her saddle bag for the mobile and called Bill's number. She yelled into the phone, telling him the situation, but she couldn't hear what he said over the pounding waves.

'Tell Woody and Vi to come!' she screamed.

'They're not going to get here in time, Sam.' Bonnie stared out to sea. 'Look! That wave went right over them!'

'Follow me.' Sam trotted Blondie above the high tide mark. She unbuckled the saddle bags and dropped them on the sand. 'No point getting all this stuff wet,' she said. 'Can you pass me that rope they left on the verandah, please?'

'You're not, Sam!' Bonnie's eyes were as big as an owl's. 'You can't swim Blondie out and save them. That was just a story.'

'We have to, Bon. We can't just leave them drowning. They all have mums and dads, maybe kids. They might even have kids at our school.' She tied the green rope onto the horn of her saddle. 'Anyway, Blondie will do it easy. And we can be heroes.'

Blondie went straight into the surf. The big waves didn't faze her at all. She swam right through them.

Pants raced up and down in the shallows, barking. Bonnie watched her friend clinging to the palomino as the waves broke over them.

'Please, Tex,' she begged. 'Please go in.' She booted him hard. 'Sam needs us.'

Tears of frustration blurred her vision as the stubborn appaloosa baulked at the shallows. But then he moved forward into the water.

'I love you, Tex!' Bonnie shouted as they crashed through the waves after Blondie.

Heroes

Blondie felt like a big, safe ship. All Sam had to do was to hang on tight. They were on the leeward side of Skull Rock, where the waves weren't so big.

'Can you swim this far?' Sam yelled to the men.

The one with the moustache gave a thumbs up. That must be Soggy, thought Sam. They pushed away from the rock on a big swell and swam towards her, two men supporting the third, who was limp and bleeding from the head. Sam felt suddenly afraid. They looked like drowned rats but they were much bigger and stronger than her. She threw the rope towards them.

'Don't come any closer!' she shouted, but they kept coming. Suddenly Blondie lunged at the swimmers, baring her big yellow teeth. With her mane wet and her ears back she looked like a dragon. 'She'll bite your face off!' Sam shouted. 'Hang on to the rope!' She turned Blondie towards

the shore and saw Bonnie and Tex just clearing
the last breaker. Tex held his chin up high.
You could see that he hated getting wet. 'You
champion, Bon!' Sam shouted, her fear ebbing.
Bonnie took the end of the rope and they towed
the drowning men to shore between them.

'Look, Sam!' Bonnie pointed. 'There's your dad!' The police car was racing along the beach. Sam dropped the rope and cantered to meet it.

'Are you all right?' Bill shouted. 'Are you both all right?'

Sam nodded. She suddenly felt teary again. A helicopter came thudding over the sand dunes and suddenly the beach was crowded. Vi and Woody's ute came screaming down the beach, the collies all barking in the back.

Bonnie and Sam rode the horses up to the sand dunes, away from the action. Blondie drew the line at helicopters. She snorted and danced as Sam slid off her. The girls leaned against each other and Pants wriggled between them.

'I'm shaking,' said Bonnie.

'Me too.' Sam showed her wobbling hand. 'But we saved them, Bon.'

Abalone explanations

The helicopter finally lifted away, taking the injured man to hospital. The other two sat with blankets around them, drinking cups of tea and telling Bill their story. For months Soggy had moored his catch of abalone to a buoy near Skull Rock then returned at night to pick them up. Last night a huge wave had swamped the

boat. 'We always use the shepherds' hut to store
dry clothes and gear. Young Lofty got a hell of a
fright last night when he found you girls there,'
Soggy said. 'But it was a good thing. We would've
been history if it wasn't for you and your horses.'

Bonnie and Sam cantered behind Vi and
Woody's ute, following them back to Banksia
Ridge. Pants ran with the collies, swerving at
seagulls. Blondie shifted into the shallows and
Tex moved with her, sending spray flying as they
raced along.

Bonnie and Sam let the horses pick at the long grass beside the road and looked down at their town. Currawong Creek was just the same.

There were no TV cameras waiting for them. Bill made sure their rescue didn't turn into a circus, and let them give just one interview to the *Currawong Creek Chronicle*.

'Janice will be pleased that we got Tex to have a swim,' said Bonnie. 'Let's go and tell her.'

BONNIE and SAM
Saving Mr Pinto

For Roddy A.L.
For Coco R.H.

Winter

Bonnie and Sam knew all the horses and ponies in Currawong Creek. They were **horse-crazy!**

Neither of the girls had their own pony but they managed to ride almost every day. They kept an eye on all the horses in town. Now, in winter, when the days were short and the nights

were long and cold, Bonnie and Sam were
always busy after school.

They stopped at Tarzan's paddock first.
Tarzan was the grumpiest pony in town but
he knew Bonnie and Sam always brought him
a treat to make him happy.

'Look at you,' said Sam as he picked up her
apple core with his whiskery lips. 'You look like
a doormat, you're so hairy.'

'That's right,' said Bonnie, scratching his ear.
'You don't even need a rug.'

Bella

Whale

Next they visited big Whale, who shared a paddock with tiny Bella, then Blondie and Tex behind the newsagency, and Horrie the old racehorse, who loved a relaxing neck massage.

Blondie

Tex

Horrie

Tricky

They stopped to check their friend Tricky,
who Bonnie once rode in a circus. Sam
straightened his rug and Bonnie threw him
a biscuit of hay from the shed.

Then they skipped along under the leaden
winter sky, jumping to keep warm and dodging
the puddles in the street. The paddocks were
bare, with clumps of jonquils and daffodils
scattered over them. The deciduous trees
had lost all their leaves. It was a cold,
grey landscape.

Rugs and rubs

The last stop before they reached Sam's house was Biscuit, a nervous chestnut mare who belonged to Wally Webster, the local stock agent. Biscuit would have frozen without the girls. Her coat was fine and she shivered in the cold weather, but Wally refused to buy a rug for her. 'It makes as much sense as putting a pair of pants on a seagull,' he had snorted. 'Horses have fur. They don't need overcoats.'

'Actually, they have hair, not fur,' Sam had whispered to Bonnie as Wally sloshed away through the puddles. They didn't want to be too cheeky to Wally because he let them ride Biscuit whenever they liked.

When Bonnie and Sam had told their riding instructor about Biscuit, she had given the girls an old rug, and now Biscuit was snug in a bright purple coat. While Bonnie gave Biscuit some hay, Sam felt around the mare's shoulders and wither, checking for rubs.

'Right as rain,' she said to Bonnie. 'I'll race you to the house!'

An offer

Sam slurped her hot chocolate and looked out the window at Drover sheltering from the wind behind the shed in her paddock. Sam's family was just her and her dad. Bill was the local policeman and Drover was his horse.

The phone rang. 'Bags not answer,' Sam said. 'It'll be your mum, wanting to pick you up.'

Bonnie lived on a big farm out of town. If she
didn't go straight home on the school bus, her
parents had to drive in from Peppermint Plain
to collect her. As she went to Sam's house nearly
every night after school, this meant a lot of trips
for Chester and Woo. But it wasn't Woo on the
phone. It was their riding instructor.

'Yep, yep, sure. Yes, we can come right away.'
Bonnie hung up the receiver. 'That was Cheryl,'
she said, her voice excited. 'She wants us to go
to her place *now*. She's got an offer for us.'

Cheryl Smythe-Tyght lived with her mother and an elderly blue heeler, called Burl Ives, on the outskirts of Currawong Creek. Everybody called their farm Tidytown because it was so neat: white fences, red sheds, green grass, straight rows of trees, and a smooth gravel drive that Bonnie and Sam raced up. Sam's little dog, Pants, ran ahead. Pants was short for Smartie Pants, because she thought she knew everything.

Cheryl's beautiful dressage horse, Chocolate Charme, nickered to them from the open stable door. He was covered in rugs, so only his ears, eyes and nose could be seen.

'Hi, Chocko!' they called to him. From time to time the girls picked up horse poo in his paddock and Cheryl paid them in riding lessons. Riding Chocko was different from riding any other horse. He was big, powerful, graceful, and had beautiful manners as well. When they rode Chocko they felt like princesses.

'How are my two lovely girls?' called Cheryl's mother. Kath had ridden show horses all her life and she liked anyone who loved horses as much as she did. She hugged them both into her fluffy purple cardigan with white stallions embroidered on it. 'Come on, Cheryl,' she said impatiently. 'Ask them!'

Cheryl looked at Bonnie and Sam very seriously. 'What I'm going to ask you will be fun, but it's also hard, responsible work.' Bonnie looked at Sam and tried not to laugh. She always got the giggles when anybody gave her a talking to. But Cheryl said, 'I'm going to the Royal Show next week. Mum's sister, Auntie Lil, usually comes and helps Mum strap for me, but she's broken her wrist and I need some extra help.' She looked at them both for a long time and Bonnie had to fight the giggles again. 'Would you two like to come and help?'

'Woohoo! Woohoo!' yelled Bonnie and Sam. They had dreamed of going to the Royal Show since they were little girls. 'YES!' they both shouted at once.

'There's something else.' Cheryl put her finger up, to quieten them.

'I entered you in the Royal Show Junior Girl Rider, Bonnie, ages ago, after you won at the Gardenhope Show.'

Best Junior Girl Rider

Every summer and autumn, Cheryl and Kath
travelled to agricultural shows around the
country, competing in hack and riding classes.
Cheryl's purple four-wheel drive towed
a matching purple horse float.
Sometimes Bonnie and Sam
went to help, and occasionally
Cheryl let the girls enter
a riding class on Chocko.
Bonnie always did better
than Sam, even though
Sam was a good rider.

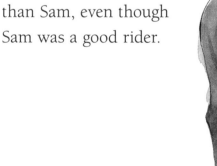

'It's just because I'm small, Sam,' Bonnie said to cheer her friend up, and that was part of it. Bonnie looked like a sprite on Chocko. But she also had a grace and magic that made her stand out. 'Star quality,' Cheryl called it. When Bonnie won Best Junior Girl Rider at the Gardenhope Show, she was ecstatic about her lovely blue sash. Sam clapped until her hands were sore. Neither of them realised that Bonnie's win had qualified her to ride at the Royal Show.

Now, Bonnie felt excited and scared at the same time. Sam felt a twinge of envy, then pushed it behind her and they both screamed with happiness.

'Next week Mum and I will go to the showgrounds and get Chocko settled in,' said Cheryl. 'I've asked your folks to let you miss the last day of term so you can catch the train into the city. Mrs Puller is bringing one of her cakes to the show and she said she'll look after you.' She smiled. 'I need you then because Chocko and I are riding in the Garryowen.'

'Mum will tell you about the Garryowen,' Cheryl said in response to the girls' raised eyebrows. 'She's ridden in it heaps of times. I'm going to feed Chocko.'

Kath pulled down a cracked photo album and flipped through it. 'Look, here I am at my very first Garryowen, forty years ago.' Bonnie and Sam peered at the black-and-white photograph of Kath, looking more like Cheryl, on a tall grey horse. 'That's old Overlander. He was my first hack.'

'What is the Garryowen, Kath?' asked Sam.

'Well,' said Kath, 'it's a competition for the lady rider and her horse, for the best in the land. There are six judges giving marks for saddlery, general appearance, rider's costume, riding, horse's manners and paces, and horse's confirmation and soundness. Everything has to be perfect.'

'Why is it called the Garryowen?' asked Bonnie. 'What does it mean?'

'I think it's a famous Irish marching tune, but it was also the name of a horse. Garryowen was

a beautiful hack owned by a famous rider called Violet Murrell, who lived about seventy years ago. That's before even *I* was born. One night Violet woke to find the stables on fire with her horses all trapped inside, including her favourite, Garryowen. She died trying to get them out and the horses all died too, and I think her husband and their little dog died later.' Kath wiped a tear away. 'They started the Garryowen in memory of Violet and her courage.'

on the train

Bonnie and Sam waved to Woo as the train creaked slowly out of Baxter Station. The railway line didn't go as far as Currawong Creek, so Woo had driven Mrs Puller and the girls to catch the train at Baxter.

'See you next week!' Woo called to them. Pants looked at them sadly from the car. She hated to be left behind.

Mrs Puller held her cake tin tightly on her lap. At every Royal Show for the last fifteen years she had won a prize for her fruit cake. She was famous in Currawong Creek for her fantastic wedding cakes. Now she stared at Bonnie and Sam through her pointy glasses.

'You won't misbehave, will you?' she said. 'I'm not used to children. Mr Puller and I were never blessed with little ones.'

Sam felt awkward. She knew Mr Puller had died last year and she didn't know what to say, but Bonnie leapt right in. Woo had taught Bonnie that people like to talk about their loved ones.

'No, Mrs Puller, we'll be good,' said Bonnie. 'Tell us about Mr Puller. Did he used to go to the show with you?'

It was as though Bonnie had unplugged Mrs Puller. Story after story came tumbling out: the time Mr Puller won the woodchop, when Mr Puller dropped the cake, Mr Puller and the runaway pig and Mr Puller's pasta disaster.

In the city

Bonnie and Sam's eyes were on stalks as the train passed through the city. In Currawong Creek everybody looked pretty much the same, but here the streets were crowded with people of all shapes and sizes, wearing clothes and hairstyles that might have been from another planet. The train moved on again, wobbling across a mesh of silver tracks.

'We'll be there soon,' said Mrs Puller. 'Make sure you've got all your bags. I know how forgetful you young people can be.'

Just before the showgrounds, the train stopped to let another train past. Sam stared idly at the leaning fence beside the railway tracks. Bulging graffiti spelt something she couldn't read. It was everywhere, writing you couldn't understand. Bonnie was thinking the same thing.

'It's like yelling but not saying anything,' she said. 'Maybe it's a secret language that only the graffiti writers know.'

Suddenly Sam saw something move behind
the fence. 'Look, Bon! There's a pony in that
backyard!'

Bonnie leapt to the window so she could
see through the gap in the fence. The pony took
a step forward and they could both see it clearly
– a tiny grey thing, with all his ribs showing.

'He's starving!' Bonnie's voice cracked with
emotion at the sight of the poor pony. He had
a dirty rope tied around his neck.

'He's tied up to the clothes line, Bon,' said
Sam. 'Look, you can see the top of the Hills
Hoist above the fence.'

Mrs Puller wriggled over so she could see, too.
She didn't let go of her cake tin.

'Oh, the poor little thing,' she cried. 'Who
could treat an animal so badly?'

The Royal Show

Mrs Puller led Bonnie and Sam through the showgrounds. She knew all the streets and alleys by heart. Music blared and motors roared as they walked past the sideshows. There were so many different noises competing that it was impossible to hear anything.

Carnival workers shouted, advertising their games; toys and show bags fluttered in the breeze; and people on the Chair-o-Plane screamed above them.

Gradually they left the noise behind them as they circled behind the huge grandstand of the main arena. The Ferris wheel loomed high above pavilions where all sorts of agricultural produce were displayed. The streets thronged with farmers leading their cattle and horses to the judging arena.

'That's where I'll be taking my cake.' Mrs Puller pointed to a pavilion down a cobbled street. 'And here you are.' She led the girls past a long building where horses poked their heads out the stable doors. At the end, Sam could see a purple horse rug.

'That has to be Chocko,' she said to Bonnie.

'Kath! Kath!' Bonnie couldn't tell the story of the poor starving pony quickly enough. Her words came out so fast that Kath couldn't understand anything. Finally, she sat on her bag and took some deep breaths while Sam explained what they had seen. Kath was like Bonnie's Aunt Birdy – she always listened and didn't treat them like little kids.

'Oh, dear,' said Kath, her blue eyes filling with tears. 'It sounds like a very bad situation.' She hugged the girls close. 'That little pony needs rescuing. Let me think about things for a while.'

Sam felt as though a heavy load had been taken from her. She wished her dad was there but if Kath said she'd think about the pony, she would, and maybe she'd know what to do.

'Cheryl's gone to buy some extra horse shampoo,' said Kath. 'So it's up to me to welcome you to Paris.' She made a bow. 'Come in, ladies, to your home away from home.'

Paris

The horses and riders competing at the Royal
Show stayed at the showgrounds for ten days.
Every afternoon at three o'clock they all took
part in the Grand Parade.

'Everybody has to be in it,' explained Kath.

The horses lived in stables and the people
lived nearby in tiny rooms called lockers. At
the end of each stable block were communal
bathrooms and toilets. Kath and Cheryl had
been coming to the show for forty years and
they always stayed in the same locker. They
called it Paris, because it had a tiny square of
lawn and a plum tree in front of it. Chocko's
stable was right next door. Cheryl and Kath
had set up a card table with an electric jug and
frying pan and some camping chairs.

'We've got folding beds,' said Kath. 'We'll
sleep down here. Your bedroom is upstairs.

And look…' She kneeled beside the wall and pointed to a wobbly drawing. 'Cheryl drew this little horse when she was four.'

Bonnie and Sam climbed up the rickety ladder, spread their sleeping bags out on the airbeds Cheryl had blown up, and unpacked their things, turning the tiny space into home.

'Look, Sam. We've got a window.' Bonnie released the latch and looked down the sloping roof to the street below. 'It's like a little town. I can't wait to explore.'

Suddenly something banged the floor from below. It was Kath, with a broom.

'I have a plan, girls,' she called. 'Come down and I'll explain it.'

'Ssshhhh! We have to be as silent as wolves.'
Kath crept along in the shadow of the
grandstand, Burl Ives at her heels. She was
dressed in black, like a cat burglar. Bonnie
and Sam wore trousers and parkas over their
pyjamas, with beanies to keep their heads warm.
It was so cold their teeth were chattering.

Sam looked back over her shoulder. If Cheryl
knew what they were up to, she'd be furious.
But this was Kath's solution to the problem
of the neglected pony and Bonnie and Sam
weren't going to argue. None of them could
bear the thought of the little pony spending one
more day in misery, yet they were all aware of
Cheryl's big event in two days time.

'We can't tell her,' Kath had said. 'It will
ruin everything for her. She won't be able to
concentrate on Chocko and the Garryowen if
she knows about the pony.'

Cheryl slept like a log, so once she began to
snore that night, Kath shook the girls awake and
they set off to save the pony.

Bonnie reckoned the backyard was only about a hundred metres away from the showgrounds station. A well-trodden path ran through the long grass that grew against the back fences and they padded along it like robbers in the night, following Kath's downturned torch.

'This is it,' whispered Sam, pointing to the silver graffiti reflecting in the moonlight. She peered through the fence into the backyard. The house was dark.

'Yes! There he is!' Kath wriggled beside her and Bonnie smelled the Chanel perfume that she always wore. Burl Ives pushed up to the gap too, whining.

'Oh, the poor little thing!' sighed Kath.

'Can we just take him?' whispered Bonnie. 'Isn't that stealing?'

'I'd call it a rescue,' said Kath. 'No pony deserves to be kept in these terrible conditions. Let's see if we can untie his rope...'

Panic!

WOOF! WOOF! WOOF!

A black shape hurtled across the yard, barking furiously at them. Burl Ives ran yelping into the night. Kath and Bonnie and Sam raced back along the track, trying not to scream, tripping and stumbling in their panic.

Suddenly a light flooded the yard and the huge shadow of a man spread out. 'Get out! Go on! Get!' The dog kept barking, a savage, growling bark that sounded like a wild beast.

The man shouted a long, loud burst of angry
swear words and the three horse rescuers and
their dog ran on without looking back.

In the safety of the showgrounds, they stopped running. Kath bent over, her hands on her knees, wheezing like a steam train. Burl Ives was panting just as loudly.

'Are you okay, Kath?' Sam asked.

Bonnie was worried, too. 'I didn't know old people could run that fast,' she said, and Kath's wheezing turned into whoops of laughter.

'Yes,' she said, between breaths. 'I'm, GASP, pretty fit, GASP, for an old girl.'

When they turned down their street they could see a light on in Paris and they knew they were in trouble.

'You WHAT?' Cheryl's eyebrows shot up in shock when she heard where they had been. She waggled her finger at Kath. 'You are the most irresponsible old lady in the world!'

Bonnie and Sam sat very still on the camping chairs, not daring to look at one another in case they got the giggles, while Kath told Cheryl the whole story. To their surprise Cheryl calmed down.

'It's very sweet that you didn't want to worry
me because of the Garryowen, but I would rather
know than have you sneaking around in the
dark.' She turned the electric jug on. 'I shampooed
Chocko twice today. He's so clean you could eat
off him. All I have to do tomorrow is give him a
light work-out and ride in the Grand Parade.' She
spooned Milo into the mugs. 'I'll have plenty of
time to help rescue the clothes-line pony.'

A bird's eye view

Bonnie and Sam held on tight to the metal bar as the Ferris wheel took them slowly up into the sky. First they could see the showgrounds, then they could see the streets outside, then they could see the whole city. The big wheel stopped to let more passengers on and Bonnie and Sam swayed like two perching pigeons, right at the

top. The train line snaked away towards the city.

'Bon!' Sam pointed. 'There's the pony.' The unhappy pony stood, head down in a muddy, messy backyard. He looked very sad.

'And, Sam,' said Bonnie, 'you can see which house it is. It's that blue house with a pile of bricks in the front yard, in the next street along from the station.

'I'm coming! Stop that knockin'!'

Fatty Phillips pushed open his front door and blinked into the bright winter light. Two little girls and two woman stood on the front step.

'Waddaya want?' he said. 'I'm not buyin' nothing.'

Cheryl got straight to the point. 'We're not selling anything.' She looked him right in the eye. 'On the contrary. We would like to buy something from *you*.'

Kath pushed forward like a terrier. 'We know you have an ill-treated pony in your backyard and we wish to buy it. If you don't agree right now to a reasonable price we'll phone the RSPCA!'

Fatty scratched his hairy belly. He had no money and no chance of getting any until next week. He didn't have to think for long.

'Deal done,' he said. 'Give us three hundred dollars and the critter's yours.'

'Two hundred,' countered Cheryl, and Kath's glare told Fatty to accept. He led them down the side of his house, past bursting bags of garbage and piles of beer bottles. They had to wait while he locked the growling dog in the house.

The pony nickered when he saw them and Kath turned on the man.

'How could you starve a pony like this?' Cheryl untied the dirty rope. 'What are you doing with it?' she asked him.

To their surprise, tears welled in his eyes. 'I bought it from a fella at the pub. I thought my ex was bringing the kids down from Queensland and I wanted to surprise them.' He looked down at his dirty moccasins. 'But they never came. I don't know nothin' about horses. He ate all the grass in the first week and after that I've been feeding him bread.'

He followed them out to the street. 'I didn't know,' he said hopelessly.

'Ignorance is no excuse,' said Kath. She handed him two hundred dollars as Cheryl led the pony away. 'I should report you to the police!'

A surprise

While Cheryl exercised Chocko and Kath had a lie down, Bonnie and Sam took the pony to the washing bay.

'He's a pinto!' Sam said in surprise as the mud washed off him. The pony was quiet and well-mannered.

'He's somebody's pet, Sam,' said Bonnie. 'He must be stolen.' It took three shampoos to get all the dirt out of his coat and finally he was sparkling black-and-white.

'Let's call him Mr Pinto,' said Sam.

While Mr Pinto munched on hay in Chocko's stable, Sam towelled him dry and Bonnie combed the knots out of his mane and tail. Every once in a while he reached around and nudged her with his nose.

'I think he likes us,' said Bonnie.

'He's got a heart-marking under his tummy, Bon,' Sam said, as she lay on her back, drying underneath him.

'Any room for us in there?' asked Cheryl. She led Chocko into the stable and let him sniff the pony. Neither horse squealed or struck out. 'I think it's love at first sight,' said Cheryl. 'I was going to find a spare stable, but maybe he can share with Chocko.'

Kath cooked fried eggs and bacon for dinner that night and they went to bed early. Tomorrow, Cheryl was riding in the Garryowen and the alarm clock was set for four o'clock in the morning. As Bonnie and Sam drifted into sleep, fireworks exploding over the main arena lit up the loft.

Not a hair out of place

Bonnie and Sam worked
like little ants, passing, fetching, carrying,
holding and helping. Chocko was like a great
big bride with everybody fussing over him.
Cheryl plaited his mane and tail so not a hair
was out of place. She sewed the plaits into place
with matching thread. Kath wiped every inch of
him with a fine cloth, polished his hooves black
and even cleaned his teeth. There was
not a speck of dust in his coat.
Mr Pinto stood quietly in the
corner chewing hay. Now
and again he smirked at
Chocko as if to say, *Man!
You look ridiculous.*

'Look at these rules.' Bonnie flipped through the Garryowen guidebook. 'The lining of your jacket has to be navy, you have to have cufflinks with chains, a white lace-edged hanky in your left-hand waist pocket, your spur has to sit on the stitching of your boot… How do you keep track of all this stuff?'

At six o'clock the street sweepers went past and the girls stopped for breakfast. Soon Chocko was saddled and it was Cheryl's turn to get ready. Her clothes came out of their plastic covers and Kath dressed her like a doll.

Finally Cheryl was ready and swung onto Chocko. Kath inspected horse and rider carefully, searching for flaws.

'You look fabulous,' she said. 'Good luck and have a great time.'

Bonnie and Sam ran ahead of Chocko as he walked towards the main arena, then waved as he walked through the gates.

'Good luck, Chocko! Good luck, Cheryl!'

Kath, Bonnie and Sam sat high in the grandstand and watched Cheryl and Chocko go through their paces. There were ten horses lined up and they all looked absolutely perfect.

'There's another two groups to be judged after this, thirty riders altogether, but they judge them in groups of ten,' Kath explained. 'When I used to compete…'

'In the olden days,' Sam joked, and Kath gave her a play punch.

'Yes, in the olden days. This was a huge event. Sometimes there were more than a hundred competitors and we all lined up together. If you were at the end of the line, you had to wait for hours and you'd certainly lost your sparkle by the time your turn came. That's why they judge it in groups now.'

One by one the riders completed their workout, following the judge's instructions and showing off their horses. Round circles, square halts, extended trots and flying changes looked easy and effortless. Chocko did everything perfectly.

When it was time for Cheryl's costume to be marked, she dismounted and stood on a square of canvas. Bonnie and Sam couldn't help laughing as the judge carefully inspected every inch of her. 'She's even looking in her ears,' whispered Sam. Two judges checked Chocko and his gear just as thoroughly.

Finally the judges lined the horses up and they stood as still as statues. Only Chocko moved, turning his head slightly towards the stables.

'He's thinking about that little pony,' Kath said. 'Oh, dear. They'll mark him down for that.'

No prize for Chocko

'We are really sorry,
Cheryl,' said Sam. 'We
didn't mean to mess up
your Garryowen.' Bonnie and Sam felt terrible.

'That's right, love.' Kath felt guilty, too. 'If we
had left that pony where he was you would have
been placed for sure. You might even have won.'

Cheryl was snipping the thread from Chocko's
plaits, undoing hours of work in a few minutes.

'I can't pretend I'm not disappointed. But I'm
disappointed with *him*.' She slapped Chocko on
the neck. 'He's the big baby who should have
behaved better.' She teased out the plaits with
her fingers and Chocko's mane stuck out in
curls. 'I hope you feel as stupid as you look,' she

said to him. 'I'll just have to work harder for next year. But we did the right thing. We had to save Mr Pinto. I'm not sorry about that.' She turned to the girls. 'Now we have to figure out what to do with him.'

Bonnie had a plan already. 'Let's make a found poster, and stick it to the stable door. He must belong to somebody.'

Bonnie and Sam worked on the poster together.

'That looks exactly like him!' Cheryl said. 'Make sure you put our address here at the show on it. I'll get some copies made at the office and you can stick them up around the showgrounds.'

Later the girls set off to put up posters.
They took turns to ride Sam's skateboard, with
Burl Ives pulling them along. There wasn't
much asphalt in Currawong Creek, but here
at the showgrounds the streets were made for
skateboarding.

They stopped to watch the performing pigs
and bought show bags and fairy floss. At the
animal nursery they fed a baby lamb and
cuddled collie pups.

That afternoon hundreds of people stopped by
their stable to look at Mr Pinto, but nobody knew
where he was from. One shifty-looking man tried

to claim him, but he didn't know what the pony's secret marking was. And when Cheryl questioned him, he backed into the crowd and ran away.

Just as they were about to shut the stable door and have a game of Scrabble, a couple stopped to read the poster. The man had a large camera and the woman reached through the door to shake Kath's hand.

'I'm Gloria Gold, from the *Daily News*,' she said. 'I think we have tomorrow's front page story here.'

Front page news

The next day Bonnie and Sam jumped out of bed as soon as the alarm went off and got Burl Ives to tow them to the milk bar so they could buy the paper.

'Look, Kath! Cheryl!' They burst into the locker. 'We're on the front page!' The photo took up half the front page of the *Daily News* – Bonnie and Sam on either side of Mr Pinto, just their faces filling the picture.

'DO YOU KNOW THIS PONY?' screamed the headline. The text below told the story and described Bonnie and Sam as 'plucky youngsters'. Kath and Cheryl read the article, then tore the page out and stuck it on the wall of the locker.

'Well,' said Cheryl, 'that's your five minutes of fame. We've forgotten something though. Tomorrow is your riding class, Bonnie. We have to get you and Chocko ready for the Junior Girl Rider.'

Sam watched while Bonnie trotted Chocko around the practice arena. The small enclosure was crowded with riders trying to exercise their horses. They all went clockwise, then, when a bell rang, they all turned and went anti-clockwise. Cheryl stood at the fence, calling instructions to Bonnie as she rode past.

'Heels down...that's good...more contact.' When a fat appaloosa kicked out at Chocko, Bonnie slowed and rode out the gate. 'Why are you stopping?' Cheryl asked. 'You both need more work.'

'I'm sorry, Cheryl.' Sam could see tears in Bonnie's eyes. 'I don't like riding in such a crowd. Everyone is so pushy. Maybe I'm not cut out to be a show rider.'

But the next day Bonnie bravely rode out onto the main arena. 'She's going to go well,' Cheryl said. 'I can feel it in my bones.'

'And look at Chocko,' Sam added. 'He looks beautiful. Perhaps he's trying to make up for the Garryowen.'

The thirty competitors in the Junior Girl Rider event rode around the judge in a circle.

'This is where showmanship comes in,' Kath said. 'If you get stuck on the outside, the judge doesn't even see you.'

The judge called riders in one by one and finally everybody was lined up. Then it was time for the workout, and each rider did the same routine, finishing with an extended canter across the arena. Some of the horses took off like rockets then didn't want to stop, but Chocko's canter was flawless. He moved smoothly into a fast, powerful stride and then eased into a soft, square halt right on the finish line. Bonnie sat on him lightly, and her legs and hands didn't move. Sam knew she would be talking to him in silent horse talk.

When the judge lined the riders up, Bonnie and Chocko were first. Sam, Kath and Cheryl stood up and clapped. Bonnie bowed to the judge and cantered a lap of honour around the arena, her blue sash shining in the sun.

TV too!

Bonnie rode Chocko into the stable, Kath shut the door and the four of them jumped up and down, grinning and squealing. Bonnie was so excited she couldn't speak, so Kath had to phone Chester and Woo to tell them the good news. Cheryl pinned the blue sash above the stable door.

Suddenly there was a knock on the door. 'Hello! Hello! Are the girls who saved the pony there?'

A group of people peered into the locker. One man had a movie camera and a glamorous woman held up a fluffy microphone.

'Hello there! I'm Sally Starlight from *It's Your Tonight*.' Her blonde hair looked like a golden helmet. 'Can we interview you about the pony?'

They crowded into the stable and set up the camera and lights. Bonnie and Sam told their story, but when Mr Pinto tried to eat her hair, Sally Starlight said they had enough footage.

'Thanks, ladies,' she said. 'And make sure you watch the show tonight.'

Later that afternoon Bonnie rode Chocko in the Grand Parade, her winner's sash tied across her chest. Sam led Mr Pinto in the parade as well, and Sally Starlight and her team shot more footage of them. The horses were paraded in small circles in the middle of the arena, and the sheep and cattle made a big circle around them. Right out on the trotting track, the harness horses and Brewery Clydesdales made the biggest circle of all. Everybody did ten laps of the arena and the spectators in the grandstands clapped and cheered.

That night they went to Kath's friend's locker. Marnie had a portable TV and they snuggled in to watch themselves on *It's Your Tonight*.

'This will find Mr Pinto's family,' said Sam. 'Everybody watches this show.'

While they waited for the programme to start, Bonnie flipped through Marnie's copy of *Horse Deals*.

'Mr Pinto was in here!' she said suddenly.
'In *Horse Deals*. Remember, Sam? When we were
in Janice's newsagency last summer?'

'That's right,' said Sam. 'You noticed him
because he looked like a black-and-white
version of Bella. Let's ring them tomorrow.'

'Here we go.' Marnie turned the volume up
and Sally Starlight's up-and-down reporter's
voice filled the little room.

Pokey Packer

Before Bonnie and Sam had a chance to phone *Horse Deals* magazine the next day, the TV crew was back at Paris. Somebody, who knew somebody, who knew the family that owned Mr Pinto, saw the story on *It's Your Tonight* and put them in touch with the TV station. The network helicopter had flown up to the mountains where the family lived, and now it landed at the showgrounds heliport. The cameras rolled as Mr and Mrs Packer and their little girl Helen raced up to peer over the stable door.

'It's him!' Helen squealed. 'It's Pokey! Oh, Pokey, I've missed you.'

Pokey Packer had been stolen from his paddock a year ago and now he could go home. Kath made cups of tea and the Packers showed them photos of Pokey, and thanked the horse rescuers for their fine work. They insisted on giving Kath the two hundred dollars she'd paid to get Pokey.

'Do you know his secret marking?' Sam asked Helen. She nodded.

'Yes, I do.' Helen traced a heart on the wall with her finger.

Back to Currawong Creek

Burl Ives sat between Bonnie and Sam on the back seat of Cheryl's four-wheel drive, making such bad smells they had to keep the windows down. Behind them in the horse float, Chocko munched hay. Pokey Packer was on his way back to the mountains.

The city turned into suburbs and the suburbs thinned and became countryside. Sam turned to Bonnie.

'I can't wait to see Dad and Pants,' she said. 'And I wonder how all the horses are.'

'I'm missing Mum and Dad, too,' Bonnie replied. 'The show was fun, but it will be nice to be back at Currawong Creek.'

Alison Lester grew up on a farm with lots of horses and cows and dogs and cats. The first time she rode a horse she was a baby in her father's arms, and she cried when she had to get off. The horses and ponies in the Bonnie & Sam books are all based on horses she has ridden at one time or another. She still lives in the country and rides her horse, Woollyfoot, whenever she can.

Roland Harvey did not grow up on a farm, and first rode a horse last week. He has discovered that horses are easier to ride and draw from a distance, because as soon as they know what you're up to they deliberately stand in funny ways. Roland would quite like to be a horse when he grows up, as long as he's a big one. He lives in the city but spends as much time as he can outdoors.